WALK WITH EVIL

WALK WITH EVIL

ROBERT WILDER

CUTTING EDGE

ISBN-13: 978-1-954840-29-4

Published by
Cutting Edge Books
PO Box 8212
Calabasas, CA 91372
www.cuttingedgebooks.com

To a good friend and old companion former Deputy Sheriff WILLIAM H. FREEMAN

CHAPTER ONE

Where the densely packed mangrove reared high on spidery legs the current ran swiftly now as the tide ebbed toward the narrow inlet and the sea beyond.

A flat-bottomed boat, with outboard motor, strained at the line tied inexpertly among the branches, and the silently racing water rippled about its bow and purled out at the stern in a gentle wake. Small pieces of wood, a polished leaf, a fleck of grey-white down from a pelican's breast spun past and Jeff Martin followed their course with his eyes, idly and contentedly interested.

The afternoon's sun hung above the blue-shadowed pines far to the west. Jeff lifted his face to its fading warmth. Fish or no fish, it had been a fine, lazy day. He reeled in from the last cast, took the live shrimp from a hook, threw it over the side and then placed the light rod carefully in the bottom of the boat. He lit a cigarette and hunched forward on the narrow seat, hands dangling between outspread knees. The tobacco bit pleasantly at his throat and his glance scanned the ragged crests of the dunes on the beach side of the river. The pounding of the surf beyond was the steady, muted throb of a bass drum. Four weeks of this, he thought. Four weeks of Florida's sun, the magic tonic of the river, the quiet friendliness of the people in the small, bleached town.

Redemption Cay. He smiled at the name. It was not a cay but only a spit of land jutting into the estuary, shielded from the Atlantic by the long island of dunes and buttressed on the opposite side by the mainland. Redemption Cay. Who named it so, and why? For that matter, he wondered, why Threadneedle

Street in London, Maiden Lane in New York, El Niño Perdido in Mexico City? He snapped the cigarette into an arc and watched as it fell. Then, he moved forward and untied the boat.

The outboard's flywheel spun beneath the starting cord and the motor wheezed with an asthmatic cough. Patiently he rewound the cord and tugged again. There was a faint gurgle from the underwater exhaust but no explosion. Then he remembered what the man who rented the boat to him had said. "Sometime you gotta goose hit a little." His fingers searched for and found the small valve on the carburetor. He tapped it gently until the odor of gasoline was strong and again jerked the length of rope. There was no rewarding chatter. He looked up and a small frown creased his brow. The mangrove bank had dropped away with alarming suddenness. He was in the middle of the river now. The boat was riding the current with a sluggish circling, but moving always toward the mouth of the inlet where the spume crested breakers were throwing themselves furiously against the ebb. His whistle was low and speculative as he measured the distance. In five or ten minutes the surf would be tearing this light craft into driftwood. Jeff Martin wouldn't break up but he could drown, and that wasn't what he had in mind for this vacation. And if he didn't drown he would still owe a man for a boat, outboard motor, bait bucket and rod and that would be vacation's end with not even bus fare back to New York. He stood up. The boat pitched crazily beneath the unbalanced weight and he sat down abruptly, clutching at the sides to save himself from being pitched overboard. You could get real stupid, he thought angrily, when you had never been any closer to salt water than a sore-throat gargle and your experience with boats was limited to the Staten Island Ferry.

The ocean's roar was louder now. Within the narrow cut of the inlet the waves hurled spray high into the air as they met the resisting current. He would never ride them out in the boat but if he went over the side and swam at an angle with the tide he might be able to make the beach.

Regretfully he untied the new pair of gum-soled, canvas shoes and, for reasons which he didn't quite understand, aligned them neatly on the forward seat. The dungarees, also new, would be dead weight. If he was going to swim it might as well be made as easy as possible. Slowly he unbuckled the belt and began to strip.

The even beat of a motor caused him to turn quickly. A hundred yards away a heavy work boat with open cockpit and high bow was moving toward him. There was a girl forward at the wheel, and she maneuvered her craft between him and the inlet with an unhurried and exasperating calm, throttling down until he had little more than steerage way.

"Hey!" He yelled his gratitude and pulled the dungarees back to his waist, buckling the belt hastily.

There was no answering hail. The girl was regarding him with an expression of mildly resigned curiosity. She shook her head unbelievingly and a full mouth pursed itself as though she didn't want any part of this. She spun the wheel, inching in until her bow nuzzled the rowboat's side.

"I watched you." She made the statement without any particular emphasis. "Don't you know better than to cast off without starting your motor first? Almost anyone would have more sense than that, even a tourist." The voice, softly accented, held no reproof or scorn, merely a weary patience as though the river were cluttered with idiots who should have stayed ashore.

Jeff glanced worriedly beyond her to the surging inlet. "If you'll give me a rope," he said, "I can hook on and you can pull me out of here, if you will."

The girl rubbed at her nose with the knuckles of a slender, deeply tanned hand. Then she shook her head slowly with a wry and incredulous grin. "You hook a ride on a truck, mister," she commented instructively. "A boat doesn't get pulled, but towed, and a rope is a line."

"Aye aye, sir." He made a mock gesture of respect, touching two fingers to his forehead.

She stared at him for a moment and then shook her head again as she went to the stern. "Catch." The line snaked across, falling into his outstretched hands. "Make it fast to the bitt forward." Her eyes brightened. "That's up front, the little iron thing."

"You don't have to be so salty," he yelled, a faint edge of annoyance in his tone.

She watched as he crept unsteadily forward and then her boat edged past, taking up the slack. When the line was taut her motor opened with a grumbling roar and the skiff's bow lifted high out of the water. She looked back once and then turned her attention to the open water separating them from the mainland.

Bracing himself against the skiff's rocking, Jeff studied the slim, sturdy back. The girl stood with outspread legs, riding easily with the rolling motion. She wore a man's plaid flannel shirt and dungarees rolled to the knees. Her hair fell dark and heavy almost to her shoulders and blew with the wind. She lifted a hand once to thrust it away from her face. He grinned a little sheepishly, feeling ridiculously large and clumsy. The rowboat, which had seemed adequate, appeared to have shrunk into a skittering chip on which he sat with a sensation of ludicrous helplessness. It was an ignominious end to a pleasant day, being hauled around at the end of a rope by a fresh kid in her teens. He began to laugh softly, admitting to himself that even a tourist should know better than to untie—cast off, he corrected himself—before starting a motor.

They came alongside the canted and weathered dock, on the end of which was built a small shack bearing a faded sign: "Norn's Landing. Live Bait. Smoked Fish. Boats For Hire." Norn, himself, stood on the dock's end watching, his head to one side, tongue thrust into a corner of his cheek.

"Bin fishin', Judy?" He caught the gunwale of the skiff with a boat hook.

"Caught it in the inlet." Her eyes widened with a burlesqued astonishment. "Headin' for the sea, it was, like one of those lemmings."

Norn shifted the quid of tobacco from one side of his mouth to the other, thrusting it against a cheek. "That's three boats an' four Yankees I owe you for." He made the calculation slowly.

"I'll throw the Yankees in for free." The girl matched his tone. "Boats are harder to come by."

"All right." Jeff stepped from the skiff to the landing stage. "You've had your fun. I'm the dumb tourist. You're the Ancient Mariner and Captain Bligh. Do I owe you anything for the tow?"

The girl turned, staring up at him with a solemn, wide-eyed interest and then she winked and her smile was warm and understanding. "No-o-o." The word was consciously drawled and accented. "It's just part of the service. Mr. Norn sends them out and, sometimes, I bring them back. Hardly a week goes by without its happening, so don't feel too bad." She touched the throttle and the boat began to slide away from the dock.

"How's the Senator, Judy?" Norn called.

Tight anger and something, Jeff thought, that was close to pain flashed in her eyes.

"If he's where I left him—locked up—he's all right. I'll say you were asking, Mr. Norn." She was exaggeratedly polite.

"You know I didn't mean hit thataway, Judy." Norn's tone was apologetic.

"I don't know how you meant it and I don't care." She seemed to be on the verge of tears. The heel of her hand slammed against the throttle and the boat all but stood on its stern as the propellers bit deeply.

Surprised, Jeff turned inquiringly toward Norn. The man was staring after the boat regretfully. He became aware of Jeff's gaze and lifted bony shoulders in a gesture of helplessness.

"I sure enough didn't mean hit thataway. Judy ought to know I wouldn't never say a thing against her nor the Senator." His head waggled unhappily and he moved up the dock with Jeff at his side.

"Who's the Senator?" Jeff asked.

"The Senator?" Norn appeared to consider the question. "No one rightly knows, I guess. He ain't really a Senator, I don't suppose. Most folks say Judy ain't even his daughter, but they're fine people an' Judy ought to know I wouldn't say a thing out of spite."

They walked slowly, their footsteps on the loose boards sounding unnaturally loud. Jeff waited for the man to continue but Norn appeared to think he had explained everything.

"Who's Judy, then?" Jeff prodded gently.

"Judy?" Norn had a trick of repeating every question. "Judy Carter. The Senator? Well, he's Senator Carter, though as I said he ain't really a Senator an' don't anyone around here ever recollect hearing his first name. He's kind of a drinkin' man, you might say, an' whenever he gets a few too many, an' that's a lot of times, he talks in a way most folks can't understand. Someone started callin' him Senator as a joke an' the name stuck. A real handsome man he is—or he was, I guess—with a big shock of white hair like them old-time politicians used to wear. The name suits him right down to the ground an' so folks never give hit up. Judy has a real time with him an' the drinkin'. When she said she had him locked up that's just what she meant. Only—" his voice softened—"that would just be her way of taking care of him until he come out of the mysteries, so to speak. Hit would be gentle, like someone would look after a sick child."

They halted before the sagging screen door leading to the dock's shack. Norn peered up at the sky. It was softly brushed with the pastel colors of approaching dusk.

"Will you be wantin' a boat again tomorrow?"

"If you'll trust me with one after today."

"Nothin' much will happen. There's usually someone around like Judy to take care of the tourists. Give the place a bad name if we was to let 'em drown." He shook his head with an irritated gesture. "I sure wish she hadn't took what I said the way she did." His lips pursed reflectively. "Judy must be about eighteen now. If I recall right the Senator come here maybe ten years ago. Judy was just a little wide-eyed, solemn youngster. The Senator was like a mother an' a father, takin' care of her. Now she's growed an' she takes care of him the best she can. They seem to have a little money; enough to get by on, at least, an' they live up in one of the marsh cricks on a houseboat the Senator bought. Well." Norn turned abruptly. "I'll have a boat if you want hit." He pushed hastily through the door and it clattered to behind him.

Jeff lit a cigarette and stood listening to the sounds of evening; a woman calling a child, the nightly wind as it hunted through dry palmetto fans, the creaking of a homeward bound cart. He walked up the narrow, shell paved road from the waterfront past rows of cottages behind their picket fences and small yards. The perfume of oleander was heavy in the air and there was a hush upon the land and water. Yellow patches of light began to appear in scattered windows. Children, late from their play, raced through gates and pounded up the low, front stoops. Now and then he caught a glimpse of women as they moved about their kitchens, laying a table for the evening meal. There was a feeling of contentment and ordered security in the scene.

He thought that there probably weren't many places such as this one left in Florida. The new highway, swinging abruptly inland some ten or twelve miles north, bypassed Redemption Cay, all but isolating it from the tourist flood. Motorists, intent upon Miami or Key West, roared southward unaware of its existence. In the beginning the community's council and merchants had protested to the Highway Commission and the State Legislature at being cut off from the main traffic artery and the dollars which were scattered to the motels, fruit markets, orange juice stands and roadside vendors of pottery and souvenirs. Their petitions were conveniently tucked away and forgotten. The few votes to be gathered from the Cay were outweighed by the larger towns.

After the original resentment had faded the little town began to draw certain pride and defiant satisfaction in its isolation. Tourists, it was generally agreed, were all right, and the business they brought was fine for some. But a man had to put up with an awful lot to get it, so maybe it was better this way. The young people drifted away to permanent or seasonal jobs. Their elders remained to fish the river, farm their few acres, and sell the products of both in adjacent towns. The few tourists who did come to the Cay were past middle age, seeking quiet. Now and then a few strays with no particular destination in mind wandered away from the principal routes and stayed for a day and night. These and a dozen or so fishermen who had been coming down for years provided a floating population. A rambling, frame hotel with its broad verandah overlooking the river's sweep survived through their patronage. So, for the most part, Redemption Cay was Florida as it had been before Henry Flagler thrust the steel of his new East Coast Railway from St. Augustine down the peninsula.

Grant Burrows, the *Globe*'s city editor, told him about the Cay. Jeff had passed up his summer vacation. For months he had been working on a series of articles covering New York City's waterfront. It had been a painstaking, carefully documented job. It had been frustrating and even dangerous at times; dangerous because he had been forced to pry the information from men who, for years, had been held silent by fear. He persisted, digging here and there into the manifold rackets, graft and terrorism which held the longshoremen, trucking companies, and steamship lines in a tight grip of ordered lawlessness. When the assignment was finished he knew he had done a good job. The evidence for indictments and a housecleaning of the unions was detailed and accurate. The *Globe* ran the series on page one daily under his by-line. Then his telephone began to ring late at night or in the early hours of the morning. Vague and unidentified voices muttered not-so-vague threats over the wire. When he told Burrows what was happening the man leaned back in his chair, gazed out of the front windows and nodded.

"Did you think the union was going to nominate you for the Pulitzer Prize? My telephone has been ringing, too. The tires on my car have been slashed. Last night someone heaved a rock into my home in Larchmont." He smiled a little wearily. "Sometimes I think that a guy who carries a torch only gets sparks down his neck."

"I don't like it." Jeff had grinned. He and Burrows understood and respected each other. "I'm too young and beautiful to die. Maybe this is bigger than both of us."

Grant had whistled thoughtfully between his teeth and peered reflectively at the ceiling. "You're a good man and it was a fine piece of work. I'm proud of it. It took guts and a real reporter. They are hard to find these days. Everyone sits around waiting for the wire service to do the job."

"Thank you, Mr. Greeley."

"You have a three-week vacation coming." Grant ignored the jibe. "Take a couple more on the house. I'll fix it with the old man. Go someplace where you can exchange that neon-light flush for a real tan."

"I don't know where to go." Jeff confessed. "I never know where to go. Usually I spend my vacation in Costello's Bar. Tim expects me there every year. He has a corner of the room called 'Jeff's Place. Where He Sang and Danced.' "

"There is a little town called Redemption Cay—how's that for a name—on the East Coast of Florida, tucked away where you'd never find it. There's nothing to do. Maybe a few native girls with lotus blossoms in their hair. I don't know for sure. My wife was always along. You could fish, lie around and maybe pick a lotus blossom or two if that appeals to you."

Jeff had glanced out of the window. A bleak rain was slanting across Manhattan from the East River. In the murky street below the pedestrians hurried miserably, their heads bent stubbornly as they pushed against the weather.

"Right now it appeals to me fine."

"Then get out of here." Burrows swung about and picked up the day's assignment sheet. "Let me know where I can reach you. There used to be a hotel there but it may be closed and you'll have to get a room in a private home." He looked up and smiled almost wistfully. "I'd like to go along."

So Jeff had come to Redemption Cay with no other purpose than to loaf and experiment with the dubious benefits of an unfamiliar, outdoor life. He had established himself in one of the hotel's large front rooms with a view of the river and the dune crested island beyond. Through his windows, drifting between fluttering curtains, the bass tone of the ocean's murmur was a constant lullaby. The hotel had the mellow, weathered air of a contented beachcomber resting in the sun. At the moment he was its only guest, left to his own devices and untroubled by the necessity of making conversation. He had picked up a copy of *The Miami Herald* on his second day in town. The pages of advertisements for the night clubs, the strip joints and general hoopla of the resort city left him unmoved. Sucker traps, he thought, and then regarded himself in a mirror with mild astonishment. He liked it here. How would Grant Burrows have known that?

Now, as he walked toward the center of town, it occurred to him that he hadn't missed New York and Costello's and hadn't even thought much about a girl until today. Judy Carter. It was a nice name. She was pretty fresh for a kid of eighteen, but then, he reflected, there weren't any kids of eighteen any more. A couple of wars had seen to that.

Main Street was a brief stretch of pitted asphalt. On either side, lining the curb, were rusted parking meters to which no one, save a stray dog, paid any attention. A movie house, chain grocery store, the inevitable five and ten which Floridians, he discovered, all called the five and dime, a couple of barber shops, drug store and a pool room made up the business section. There was a bar and grill. "The Fish Shack. Where You Can Get Fried." This was the local sin spot, its snake pit, complete with juke box, pinball machine and a shiny bar along which were ranged stools, padded in artificial red leather. It appeared to be the town's most successful enterprise.

On his first evening Jeff had sought it out as instinctively as a salmon climbs a fall. A couple of martinis before dinner, the comfortable fraternalism of a familiar scene. Behind the bar a lean and rangy youth lounged against the shelves. He wore jeans, a bright red shirt and a Texas Stetson, creased and rolled until it was little more than a narrow wedge. He was picking his teeth absently and nodded as Jeff settled himself upon a stool.

"A dry martini."

The boy's fingers ceased probing within the cavity of his mouth and Jeff became aware of the fact that half a dozen or so beer drinkers looked up in unison, regarding him with mild astonishment.

"All right." He grinned. "I'll take a beer."

The youth thrust his hand into a box and pulled out a dripping bottle. As he wiped it he asked. "Whiskey chaser?"

Jeff lit a cigarette, taking his time. He was being kidded because of the martini. "I thought it was the other way 'round. Whiskey with a beer chaser."

The bartender snapped the metal cap from the bottle. "I just wanted to hear what you'd say." He whinnied with a high note of amusement and a ripple of appreciative laughter ran the length of the bar.

"All right." Jeff played it straight. "Make it a whiskey chaser. Bourbon."

It was a nauseating combination in that order, but he finished his beer and then tossed down the short whiskey without wincing. He laid a dollar on the bar, swung off the stool and strolled toward the doorway.

"Mister?" The bartender called.

"Yeah?" Jeff turned.

"I'll say one thing." The boy leaned earnestly over the counter. "I'm dogged if you don't make an impression."

Suddenly Jeff felt good. He had been ribbed a little, maybe. But, and this he understood, there had been no malice. He laughed. "So does that combination. I'll have to remember to tell someone I don't like about it. Good night."

Surprisingly enough there was a faint chorus of replies from the men at the bar and he had walked back to the hotel no longer feeling alien. He spoke and was spoken to by the strangers he passed. That wouldn't happen in New York. If you said good evening to people on the street they'd freeze or stare wonderingly, afraid to answer. Now he was an accepted member of The Fish Shack's club. This meant no one intruded if he didn't feel like talking but that he could join in the general conversation of sports, politics, women and wars if he was so inclined.

He turned into the place now. It was the off hour. The early drinkers had already left and the late regulars were trying to think of excuses which would get them out of their houses after supper. Bud, the bartender, glanced from an outspread comic book.

"How you, Mr. Martin?"

"Hi, Bud."

At the end of the bar a solitary figure looked up. This was a large man, heavy of shoulder, half bent over the imitation mahogany with a brooding intensity. The fingers of both hands moved aimlessly around an empty shot glass, turning it slowly. Their eyes met for a moment and Jeff was made uncomfortable by the undefinable sadness that lay as a shadow upon the face. He shifted his glance uncomfortably. This was the Senator. Norn's description had been accurate from the great, shaggy head, the air of complete detachment. There was a dignity in the figure, though, that persisted and transmitted itself despite the fact that the man had long ago passed through an alcoholic glow and was now moving uneasily within a fog.

"The hotel called here a couple of times." Bud swiped at the bar in front of Jeff. "Said if you was to come in to tell you a New York call was waitin'. You're to ask for operator fifty-four."

"Thanks." Jeff replied almost absently. Something about the Senator, half obscured in the dim light, was naggingly familiar. He worried at the memory for a moment, unaware of the faint scowl of puzzled reflection that twisted his features. "Thanks, Bud." He repeated but made no move to leave his seat.

"There's a phone booth up in front." Bud was disappointed that his message had evoked so little interest.

"All right, Bud." He lit a cigarette as his mind worked slowly backward, searching for a name, a scene, an incident to which he could link that face. I know him, he thought. From somewhere, sometime I know him. Unconsciously he shook his head.

"Young man." The voice boomed as an echo in a deep cavern. "I'll have just a little more of this excellent whiskey."

Now Jeff was sure. The rich timbre of the carefully articulated words brought a certainty but no recognition. Involuntarily he glanced again down the bar. The Senator inclined his head without a change of expression. "You, sir?" The invitation was without warmth, all but impersonal.

"Have one on me," Jeff said.

A faintly bitter smile touched the man's lips. "It matters little who pays, sir, since we shall both be indebted to the distiller."

"This here is the Senator." Bud made the introduction respectfully. "Senator, this here is Mr. Martin. He's a tourist."

"The whiskey, young man." There was no impatience in the command. "I should judge that Mr. Martin is sufficiently acquainted with barroom etiquette to introduce himself should he feel so inclined. Men go to a bar for many reasons, not the least of which is a desire to escape their fellow creatures."

Jeff had seen too many drunks to mistake the degree. The Senator was boiled, saved from pitching on his face by the fact that he had wedged himself into the corner between bar and wall. Yet, the diction was flawless; without unction, the words formed effortlessly from long practice. He tapped a knuckle thoughtfully against his teeth, trying to remember something.

"What'll it be, Mr. Martin?"

Bud's question interrupted his thoughts. "I'll take a little bourbon and plain water."

"Don't you want to know what that call is about?" Bud set the bottle on the bar and watched as Jeff poured.

"It can wait a few minutes." He lifted his glass in the Senator's direction. "Your health," he said mechanically.

The Senator shook his massive head admonishingly. "Of all the things we may get from this whiskey, sir, health is least likely. I have always considered that to be the most nonsensical of toasts. Confusion, damnation, an addled brain, a diseased liver; those are the things we might logically expect. To say health, happy days, good luck only argues words without thought."

Jeff grinned. "Oblivion!"

"That, sir, I'll drink to." The Senator regarded him approvingly and his whiskey disappeared in a single swallow. He took a soiled bandanna from a hip pocket and touched his lips fastidiously.

Jeff finished half of his drink and then swung away from the stool, searching his pockets for a dime as he went down the room toward the telephone booth.

He dialed long distance, gave the girl the information on the call, waited while the circuit was set up. He wondered what Burrows wanted. It had to be Grant. No one else knew where he was; a girl or two, maybe, but a call from one of those would be collect. He looked at his watch. It was half past five. The final edition had been in for an hour. Grant would be calling from home, since he usually left his desk at four.

"Jeff?" Burrows' voice almost startled him.

"Yes, Grant?"

"Where the hell have you been?"

"On vacation." He closed the door. "What's up?"

"Do you remember Edward Valenti?" Grant didn't waste time with pleasantries.

"Sure, like I remember Capone or Legs Diamond. But I was only a child, you remember; just a slip of a boy running copy on the *Trib*. He went to Alcatraz on a ten to twenty, didn't he?"

"That's right." From a distance of fifteen hundred miles Grant Burrows patted him on the back. "He was released yesterday. No one could get near him when he came out. A car with a couple of his boys met him. He got aboard a private plane. No one has been able to check his whereabouts after that."

"So?" Jeff knew what was coming.

"So. Find him for me."

"You're kidding. It's a real big country."

"I'll narrow it down a little for you. I have a tip that he's in Florida; Palm Beach, to be exact. Happy now?"

"No."

"If I were you I'd run down to Miami. Drop in on one of the sheets there and go through the clips on Valenti. It'll refresh your memory. As you said, you were only a slip of a lad, eager to work for Grant Burrows one day. I could have you filled in from here but the other way is quicker and easier."

"What about my vacation, those fish and native girls you told me about?"

"You're warm, aren't you?"

"Yes."

"The sun is shining?"

"Not at the moment."

"The days are pleasant beneath azure skies and a million people wish they could be in Florida, isn't that so?"

"Yeah, yeah, yeah." Jeff was resigned.

"Well." The words were crisp now. "We're freezing here. There is slush eight inches deep on the streets. I have to wear galoshes, a muffler and overcoat. Tomorrow it is going to rain turning to sleet. What are you complaining about?"

"Nothing, Mr. Burrows. But, all I can say is that you have the shortest memory I know of. 'Go ahead,' " Jess mimicked accurately, " 'Take your vacation and a couple of weeks on the house. You're a real good boy and I'm proud of you. Rest and be happy.' "

Burrows ignored the complaint. "By the way. The tip is exclusive."

"Where in Palm Beach?" Jeff deliberately made his voice sound weary knowing it would irritate Grant. Actually he was interested. "There's Palm Beach and West Palm Beach."

"That's right." Burrows's sarcasm was deceptively mild.

"Well? Which side and who does he know down that way?"

"Santa Claus." There was an abrupt click as Burrows hung up and broke the connection.

Valenti? Jeff sat for a moment in the dark cubicle. In its time the name had been as well known as Dutch Schultz, Capone, Dillinger. He pushed at the folding door. Valenti. He was an old man now, an anachronism, a shadowy survivor of another era. A feature story, maybe, but he was not news. Who was there to remember Valenti or even care? He grinned wryly. Grant Burrows remembered, and what Burrows wanted Burrows got, even if it meant pulling him off a vacation. Tomorrow he'd take a bus down to Miami and see what could be dug out of the clips that might give him a lead on where Valenti would go.

At the bar again he finished his drink, peering thoughtfully into the empty glass.

"Bad news, Mr. Martin?" Bud was not to be denied his portion of a call from New York.

"No." He looked up, shaking his head. "I'll have another bourbon." He glanced down the bar. The Senator's head was drooping. It jerked spasmodically now and then as the man was snatched back to consciousness. The eyes were lusterless, dulled by a compelling drowsiness.

"I sure wish he'd go home," Bud whispered as he put out a fresh glass. "Judy'll give me fits if she finds him here. Always acts like it was my fault. What am I supposed to do? A man comes in I gotta serve him."

"Young man." The words swelled as a deep chord. "Stop whispering over me to a comparative stranger." The head lifted slowly. A small, regretful smile touched the lips. "It is quite true, sir, as you can see. I am drunk. This is a condition which, for one reason or another, always alarms our young friend there. He indulges in futile lamentation."

"Well," Bud spoke defensively. "It's only because of Miss Judy, Senator. She just jumps all over me, like I was responsible."

"That, my dear young man, is an occupational hazard which all bartenders must recognize. You should meet it bravely and without flinching."

Bud shrugged and lifted his eyes toward the ceiling and then grinned helplessly. Listening, Jeff was astonished that anyone so far gone with liquor could enunciate clearly. On the surface the Senator was a familiar enough type. The loquacious rummy with a delight in the sound of his own words. Yet there was something more. The Senator spoke from some deep loneliness. Words alone, the reassurance of speech, were assuasive.

The door opened and a couple of men walked in. They were townspeople, greeting Bud and waving to the Senator.

"How you, Senator?"

He nodded and turned again toward Jeff. "Men drink for many reasons, Mr. Martin, but all of them are escape, the dark current on which a man may drift into oblivion. To find out why he drinks it is necessary to know only from what he runs. That, gentlemen, is my thought for the day." With an effort he rose from the stool, lurched heavily and caught at the bar, almost falling, hanging precariously to the edge.

Jeff moved quickly to catch his arm, feeling the helpless weight as the Senator sagged against him. He looked at Bud.

"Give me a hand." He called angrily. "Can't you see he's out on his feet. Where does he live? Can you get there in a cab?"

Reluctantly Bud came down and took the Senator's other arm. "You can get to the edge of the crick. After that you gotta walk maybe a hundred yards an' he sure can't walk."

"Well, we'll get to the edge of the creek, then."

The Senator mumbled quietly. Holding him between them they inched toward the door and outside. A cab was parked across the street and Jeff whistled sharply. The Senator weaved with the slow, ponderous movement of an uneasy elephant. He was doubly heavy in his helplessness.

The taxi driver grinned understandingly as he drew abreast and then reached back to open the door.

"Do you know where he lives?" Jeff was impatient, angry at having been maneuvered into this situation.

"Sure."

With Bud's assistance he half rolled the Senator through the door and on to the seat. Then he followed, pushing the man into a corner where he slumped, snoring with a soft, wheezing sound. Jeff looked at him and felt his irritation mount. A real rummy.

The car racketed down Main Street and then into a side road that skirted the waterfront. Buttressing the Senator with a shoulder to keep him from sliding to the floor Jeff lit a cigarette. In the match's glow the man's face was briefly illuminated. He studied the features and then shook his head, puzzled. There was something dimly remembered there but he could not name it.

"He's a real character, the Senator is." The driver half turned. "I guess he's the only man I ever saw who could look like he's standin' up when he's fallin' down."

"Uh!" Jeff grunted, discouraging conversation.

The road straggled along a slight ridge and then dipped to the flat land along which the marsh grass was high and pungent with the odor of muck, warm and brackish. Small canals wound themselves in dark and silent streams toward the river. There was a movement beside him and he turned as the Senator struggled into an upright position.

"This is gracious of you, sir." The words were distinct.

Jeff looked at him in amazement. A moment ago he had been asleep, passed out. Now he sat almost straight and only the uncertain movement of a hand across his lips betrayed him.

"You certainly come out of it in a hurry."

"I am never quite out of it, sir." The Senator smiled feebly. "At the moment I can place a certain amount of trust in my brain, but my legs, I fear, would betray me."

"Do I know you, Senator?" Jeff asked abruptly. "I have a feeling that I do."

"Unfortunately, sir—Martin, isn't it? Well unfortunately, Mr. Martin, our acquaintance is as short as the Fish Shack's bar. However, we progress. You in the role of a good but reluctant Samaritan. I, momentarily, in need of succor."

Jeff grinned and shook his head admiringly. "How do you sober up so fast?"

"I am far from sober, Mr. Martin. Do not mistake a certain alcoholic cunning for sobriety."

"Well, if you're not sober, it's a reasonable facsimile."

"The real test approaches rapidly." The Senator extended a hand. Beyond it a light, lemon-yellow against the darkness, appeared suddenly over the marsh. "We must soon negotiate a path filled with traps and deadfalls and a plank from shore to houseboat. If I make that, with your assistance, of course, we may concede that I am reasonably sober. The idea is slightly terrifying."

The road ended abruptly in a small clearing ringed by the patches of high and slender reeds that swayed and bent upon each other as a faint breeze swept their tips. Beyond, Jeff could see the houseboat moored close to the shore. The cab quivered to a halt and he slid out, extending a hand to the Senator who seemed unwilling to face what lay outside the compartment. Finally he sighed.

"I suppose so, Mr. Martin. It is the large coin with which I pay for so little pleasure." He thrust himself forward, holding to each side of the door, ignoring Jeff's proffered hand. On the ground he planted both feet as though to root himself into the earth.

"You want some help, mister?" The cab driver called.

"A leash for your tongue, sirrah!" The Senator struck an unsteady pose and then he grinned and winked at Jeff with the broad humor of a boozy Puck. "Mr. Barnheart is quite an admirer of the fluent but senseless tongue. But let us be at the business of negotiating the few remaining but hazardous yards together."

"Wait for me," Jeff called over his shoulder.

"I ain't got no place to go, mister." The driver was comfortably draped through the open window, watching them. "Take your time."

With the Senator threatening to carom off him at any moment into the muddy ditch, Jeff braced himself, taking the unsteady burden of weight as his feet reached cautiously along the path to where double planks spanned the water between shore and boat. He paused and regarded the narrow footbridge dubiously. Below it the water lay dark, silent and uninviting.

"I don't think we're going to make it, Senator."

"Nonsense, Mr. Martin. Don't be of faint heart. Put your confidence in me, grasp my hand in this new friendship. I always make it. Well, almost always. Should misadventure overtake us we will cry with the ancient warrior: 'Stranger! Tell Sparta that here by her command we died!' "

A door, below the deck's level on the houseboat, opened and an oblong of light was laid out, partly illuminating the gangway. Within the door's frame the girl, Judy, stood, listening.

"Judy, my child," the Senator called with hopeful reassurance. "We have a weary traveler at our gate. Summon the minstrels and fetch a torch to guide us."

The slender figure stiffened. "How did you get out?" The question was softly voiced and carried a note of weary patience.

"I had the handmaidens of guile and duplicity at my side."

"I sure didn't know they had keys to the doors I locked." She moved forward, outside the light, and stood by the railing, peering at the shadowy figures. "Just leave him alone," she called to the darkness. "One of you is about all I can handle. Just go on home and leave him alone." A tight anger was in her voice.

"Tut! Tut! my child. Fie. For shame." The Senator broke from Jeff's encircling arm and with a surprising display of agility sprinted across the boards and flung himself upon one of the two-by-four pillars supporting the roof. His arms wound about it. "There, Mr. Martin!" He shouted triumphantly. "That is how it is done." The words trailed off as though sleep had suddenly overcome him.

As Jeff watched, the man, still clinging to the post, began to slide almost imperceptibly until he lay, finally, in a large, formless heap on the deck, his arms holding the post lovingly. Jeff was tempted to swing about and walk away. Then he remembered an obligation. She had all but fished him out of the river a few hours ago, and the Senator was too heavy for her to handle. He strode over the planks and stood within the light.

"Oh!" There was surprise in her voice. "It's you."

The Senator snored with the sound of burbling water. Jeff bent down and unlocked the clutching arms. Then he dragged the burden across his back in an imitation of a fireman's hold and raised himself into a half-standing position.

"Tell me where to put him." He kept his voice softly sympathetic.

"I suppose you bought it for him." The accusation flared. "He didn't have any money. I hid it. Someone had to buy it."

"I didn't buy it for him, and in case you've never tried to carry him he's heavy. Now tell me where you want him or I'll drop him on the deck." He was furious; women were always the same. Wives or daughters, they invariably blamed the one who brought their men home.

"Inside." She crossed to stand before the open door. When he moved unsteadily toward the opening she ducked down and into the cabin and waited as he shambled in. "Here." She nodded toward a bunk. "Just put him there." The voice was softened. "Please."

With a prodigious effort, stimulated by anger, he rolled the Senator into the berth and then straightened up. She was regarding him with a wide-eyed, unhappy contriteness, and he was abruptly no longer annoyed. He smiled comfortingly.

"I'm sorry." She spoke slowly. "It's just that I— sometimes—" She shook her head quickly, unable to continue, and then went to the bunk. For a moment she looked down at the sleeping figure and then tenderly pulled a folded blanket over it, patted the shrouded form and drew Pullman-style curtains to close the berth. When she turned she stared at Jeff. A tiny, unhappy smile touched her lips. "He'll be all right now. I—I have to take it out on someone when he gets this way. I guess I just want to blame someone else, not him."

Jeff was embarrassed. He glanced about the cabin. It was bedroom, dining and living room and kitchen in one. The nickeled kerosene lamp cast a subdued light, warming the copper pots hanging upon walls and glistening on the waxed leaves of ivy that trailed from them. The linoleum was worn but polished and freshly laundered curtains were stiff as they framed the windows. When he caught her eyes fixed upon him he nodded approvingly.

"It's nice. Feels like a home."

"It is, most of the time." Unhappiness clouded her face. "He isn't always this way, no matter what people say." There was pride and defiance in the statement.

"Is there anything more I can do?"

"No. It's all right. Thanks again. I'm sorry I yelled." She brushed past and went through the door to the deck.

The night was moistly soft, a dark, wavering cloak spread over the marsh. In the still waters of the canal the stars were transplanted, reflecting with a frosty glitter. A whippoorwill called with its sad and plaintive note. They stood by the low railing, not speaking, caught in the quiet enchantment. Beyond the marsh the few lights of Redemption Cay were a pearly aurora. A mullet leaped and fell back into the water with a plopping sound. Jeff felt the girl's arm touch his and the tremor of her body was that of a frightened puppy. It was as though, out of a sudden, aching loneliness she had drawn closer to a stranger. He had an almost irresistible desire to put his arm about her shoulders, and found himself doing just that. She didn't move.

"I don't know your name."

"It's Jeff. Jeff Martin."

"I'm Judy."

"Yes. I know."

Their voices were muted, the tone communicating something beyond the sterile words. Finally she sighed.

"I'll walk you back to the taxi." She turned from his arm and looked up into his face.

He grinned. "That's Rebel talk, like saying: I'll carry you down the road a piece."

The cab was a squat silhouette in the gloom but as they approached it along the path the headlights were snapped on and the twin beams slashed at the night.

"You get him to bed all right?"

Both Jeff and Judy ignored the question but he could sense her outrage and the sudden squaring of her shoulders as she halted.

"Thank you again." She hesitated. "I have to go back now." Words had become difficult for a reason neither could explain.

"I have to go into Miami tomorrow." Jeff wondered why he should tell her that. "What I mean is when I get back I'd like to see you again."

"I'm usually somewhere around the inlet, catching tourists."

"There ought to be an easier way. I mean, like my just walking you down the road a piece or maybe going to the movies. Or just settin' on the end of a dock an' whittlin'."

"Ah don' think Ah evah went a-whittlin' with ary man befoah, Mistuh Martin." She stared at him gravely. "An' Ah thank you kindly foah th' offah." She put her hand out. "Good night again."

The clasp was firm, the hand strong but soft. He held it a moment longer than necessary. "Ah'll be whistlin' aroun' youah stoop, Miz Judy, jus' as soon as Ah evah git back from Miami."

"You sound like Amos and Andy." She threw the words back over her shoulder as she ran lightly down the path.

On the way back to town Jeff listened absently as the taxi driver attempted to capture his interest with tales of the Senator's more memorable encounters with the bottle. Finally, sensing that he had an unappreciative audience, the man snorted and became silent. He did not speak again until they were on Main Street.

"You want to go on back to the Fish Shack?"

"No. Take me to the hotel."

"Yes, sir." He was injured and elaborately polite. "Yes, sir. Whatever you say."

In his room Jeff poured himself a drink in a water tumbler and stood by the windows, listening to the hushed growl of the ocean. For the first time in his life a woman had touched him deeply. There had been plenty of girls; sleek, poised, bright young things you met at cocktail parties or in Madison Avenue bars. He shook his head. This one was sunlight and quick shadow, the clear, crisp sparkle of the sea. Even in dungarees and a man's flannel shirt she was an awful lot of girl. He wondered about her as she must be sitting now, alone on the houseboat's deck or in the cabin, with the Senator snoring in his bunk. He swallowed part of the drink. Carter. Senator Carter. The name meant nothing, but the face and the voice were familiar.

He shrugged, put aside the glass and went downstairs to supper.

CHAPTER TWO

T*he city editor* of the Herald, in Miami, returned Jeff's press card with a pleasant nod and indicated a chair beside his desk.

"What can we do for you, Mr. Martin?" He was politely attentive.

"I'd like to go through your clips on Edward Valenti and make some notes."

"We had some AP on him yesterday when he was released." His expression was quizzically interested.

"I am, or was, on vacation." Jeff grinned. "My desk called me."

"Your desk is a long way from Miami?" It was a question.

"Valenti is not in Miami, if that's what you mean."

The man smiled understandingly. "That's what I meant."

"Well, you know how it is. A city desk gets an idea."

"Say, maybe, an idea that Valenti is in Florida?" They sparred warily but with good nature.

Jeff weighed his reply for a second. Burrows had said that the tip was exclusive. "As I said," he finally hedged, "it's only an idea of the city desk so I want to do a little checking."

The man nodded, swung about in his chair and called a copy boy. "Get the clips on Valenti." He scribbled the name on a slip of paper. "Give them to Mr. Martin here and find a place where he can work for a while."

Jeff stood up. "Thanks."

"Valenti doesn't seem important any longer but I guess that depends on where he is, who he is with, and what he's doing."

"It might," Jeff conceded. "I don't know myself."

"Well, good luck." The man smiled pleasantly and returned to a stack of galleys on his desk.

Jeff followed the copy boy, knowing that the *Herald* wouldn't leave it there. If Valenti was in Florida and news to a paper in New York, it was bigger news to a newspaper in Miami.

The file on Valenti filled two large manila envelopes. Some of the clips were so old that they had yellowed and become crisp. Jeff handled them carefully, reading methodically.

The story of Edward Valenti followed a familiar pattern: a tough young hoodlum working his way up and out of New York's teeming East Side in the early twenties. He began to make news on his own after the St. Valentine's Day massacre in Chicago. There were rumors then that he had been one of the guns behind the operation that had startled even Chicago.

As the pile of read clippings mounted at Jeff's left hand, the stature of Valenti increased. It grew as the competition was erased. The early photographs indicated that he was now going to a tailor. Gone were the tight-waisted, exaggerated-shoulder suits, the snap-brim hats. Valenti, impeccable, unsmiling, composed and a little contemptuous, appeared at nightclubs, the race and dog tracks, the ball park. Capone finally went to Alcatraz on an income tax evasion conviction and Valenti took over Chicago. Then he went to New York and the design was repeated. Crime had become big business. It sat behind desks in paneled offices. It met with a board of directors. It manipulated millions in wire rooms, policy slips, dope and girls from New York to Los Angeles, from Texas to Minnesota. The machine-gun killings were as anachronistic as the holdup of a Wells Fargo pony express rider. Valenti appeared at political dinners, was photographed at first nights. He was a shadowy but dominant personality in a nether world and inquiries were met by a shrug and the laconic statement that he was a businessman. No one could pin anything on him, not even the Internal Revenue

Bureau which received his tax returns, meticulously detailed by a reputable firm of accountants.

Jeff sent out for a container of coffee and a hamburger. The stuff he had read was part of a legend, something out of a gaudy, tempestuous, almost unbelievable era. It had been retold many times through the movies of Edward G. Robinson and James Cagney. A new generation with its eyes set upon spaceships, ray guns and H-bombs would smile tolerantly. What had occurred in the twenties and thirties was small stuff. Dropping the empty cup and crumpled tissue into a basket he turned again to the clippings and paused over an eight-column banner. MILLION DOLLAR HEIST in Brooklyn. Skimming through it, Jeff was puzzled. There was no mention of Valenti in the story, and yet it had been included in the Valenti file. He lit a cigarette and pondered.

The story ran for weeks. It started with a pushcart peddler who wheeled, beneath his assortment of sleazy merchandise, three submachine guns. It ended with the complete disappearance of an armored car and something over a million dollars. The car, after being looted, had apparently been cut into junk with acetylene torches and disposed of piecemeal. The guards and drivers were never found.

Everything pointed to a carefully planned maneuver behind which were brains and a great deal of patience. A phrase, "The Syndicate" appeared in the stories. Jeff smiled to himself. Rewrite men always had a particular fondness for those two words. The syndicate. Half the time they didn't know what it meant. The syndicate didn't need to risk the hijacking of a bank truck. The chances were that it was only carrying the syndicate's money. On the surface the robbery appeared to be a renegade operation in which some of the boys went off on their own. The syndicate was as interested as the police but for a different reason. This was bad public relations. It brought too many persons around asking questions. It would have annoyed Valenti but he would have wanted to take care of the ambitious underlings in his own way.

Jeff shuffled a handful of clippings, stacked them neatly before turning to a fresh batch. Then he whistled slowly between his teeth and felt a thin edge of excitement. He stared at a picture on a story and then re-read the head: JUDGE AMOS CARTRIGHT DISAPPEARS.

The name was Cartright but the features—younger then, grave, disciplined and clear—were unmistakably those of Senator Carter of Redemption Cay.

For a long time he studied Judge Amos Cartright and then, from his memory, began to put together the small pieces of the story. It wasn't good enough. He tagged a passing copy boy and asked for the Amos Cartright file. He tossed aside the early stuff, working toward the clips which would correspond with the date of the judge's disappearance as noted in the Valenti story. Then he matched them up and a picture began to emerge.

The armored car robbery had been a federal case and the FBI ran it down. Four men were picked up in as many parts of the country, indicted, and brought to trial. Throughout the questioning they insisted that they alone had been involved. They displayed an almost complete indifference to the proceedings of the trial. It was almost as though they were certain that the charges would be whittled down, that big money and influence were at work on their behalf. Not until the jury brought in a guilty verdict did they begin to crack up. Singly and together they began to tell the story. Two of the car's guards had been implicated. From there names of others and the syndicate poured out and among them the imperturbable Edward Valenti. They were brought to trial separately. Two were acquitted, four went to prison for life on a murder charge, although the bodies were never found, and Edward Valenti one day stood before Federal Judge Amos Cartright and heard himself sentenced to from ten to twenty years on a conspiracy and accessory charge.

Judge Cartright left the bench, retired to his chambers, changed from his robe, walked from the courthouse, and disappeared. A servant at the apartment he maintained on West End Avenue said that the judge had telephoned, saying he was going to the country for a few days. For that reason the man had not been concerned by his absence. Not until a week later, when there had been no word from Judge Cartright, had the servant communicated with the authorities....

Jeff went through the clippings again. In none of them could he find any mention of a Cartright daughter, although Amos Cartright had been married and divorced.

Jeff sat, elbows on the desk, chin propped on fists. He shook his head with a wry incredulousness. After all these years, with little effort, almost by accident, he had the solution to the mystery of Judge Cartright's disappearance in his hands. It would knock Grant Burrows right out of his chair. His fingers unclasped and stretched toward the telephone. Then they drew back; he didn't want to call New York from here, and there were a lot of questions to be answered before he could give Burrows the complete story. A bulletin, a flash to the effect that Judge Cartright had been living all these years in a small town in Florida would do nothing more than send every reporter in the state to Redemption Cay. Also, and the idea began to crystalize, the disappearance of Amos Cartright was tied in with the sentencing of Edward Valenti. Without reasoning it out, he was sure this was so. Also, what had happened to the million dollars taken from the truck? There was nothing in any of the stories to indicate that it had been recovered. He reached for the telephone again and when the operator answered he asked her to get Grant Burrows at the *Globe* and reverse the charges.

With the receiver cradled on his shoulder he lit a cigarette, listening while the operator completed the circuit and Burrows came on.

"Did you locate him?"

"No. Do you think I'm Sherlock Holmes? I'm at the *Herald* in Miami."

"Well, thanks for letting me know. I was worried, dear." Burrows was honey-sweet.

"Grant, whatever happened to the money that was taken in that Brooklyn armored-car holdup?"

The silence at the other end of the wire told him that Burrows was alert, his shrewd mind working rapidly, assaying the question, delaying the answer until he had figured out why it had been asked.

"It was never found." The reply came slowly. "What have you got?"

"I have to sit on it for awhile, Grant."

"Like, maybe, in the sun in Florida?"

"Like, maybe, in the sun in Florida." Jeff repeated the words without mockery, understanding Burrows would know what he was talking about.

"I see."

"Tell me something else," Jeff asked quietly. "Did you ever hear that Judge Amos Cartright had a daughter?"

The low whistle emitted between Grant Burrow's teeth some fifteen hundred miles away was faintly audible.

"You're kidding, Jeff?" There was something close to awe in the question.

"Uh-uh. Tell me about a daughter. I can't find any mention of a child in the clips here."

"As far as I know it was a short and childless marriage. The divorce was amicable. She was a young opera singer at the Met, no diva, no prima donna, just a young kid working her way up in small roles. I guess she never made it because I can't even remember her name now. Are you sure you don't want to tell me anything more?" Burrows was as near to being impressed as it was possible for him to be.

"No. You wouldn't let it hatch and it's all one egg."

"I could fire you. You know that. I could fire you and send another man down."

Jeff laughed. "He wouldn't know where to look. Neither do I but at least I have a starting point. Besides, I could probably get another job here on the *Herald*."

"I guess you could at that, kid. Go ahead. Take all the time you want. The weather won't begin to get nice up here for a few months yet. I sure don't want you to get your feet cold. Just drop me a picture postcard now and then. I'll understand."

"I'm going up to Palm Beach this afternoon. Any contacts?"

There was a moment's silence. "Stay away from the newspapers there."

"I intend to. Give me someone else."

"Deputy Sheriff Bill Longworth. Tell him hello for me. We used to fish together."

"Thanks."

"Jeff?" Burrows was wheedling. "Are you sure you don't want to give me anything now?"

"If I did it would spoil it. Will you believe me? I'm not holding out, I just don't know it all yet."

"Okay." The assent came reluctantly. "I suppose I ought to know when I have a good man on a story. That's what I get paid for. Do it your way. So long."

Jeff replaced the receiver in its cradle, gathered up the loose clippings and replaced them in their envelopes. On the way out he stopped by the city editor's desk.

"Find what you were looking for?"

"Background, mostly." Jeff nodded. "Thanks for your help."

"Drop in any time."

Jeff hesitated. "I'm going to need to rent a car for a few days. If I need a local reference will it be all right to give your name?"

"Sure. Tell them to call me." He smiled briefly. "I think maybe I'll put a man on your tail. I'm beginning to get interested."

"So am I. Thanks again."

Outside, in the bright, warm sunshine he walked toward Flagler Street, crossed it, and eventually found a car rental agency. He settled on a new model convertible and a few minutes later was on the main highway, driving north past seemingly endless rows of motels. He wondered idly how any of them could pay off; there couldn't be that many tourists.

As he threaded his way through the traffic it occurred to him that he didn't have the slightest idea what he wanted to know from Valenti, assuming he could find him and he would talk. Then the image of Judy Carter flashed into his mind. Who was she? Where had she come from? The man, Norn, said that the judge had come to Redemption Cay when Judy was little more than a baby. Why would a man, intent upon disappearing, burden himself unnecessarily? A child and a wife would have been a good cover but a man alone with an infant would inevitably attract attention. Also, how did you go about getting a baby? It wasn't simple. He frowned. It didn't add up, and yet he was certain that it should. Somehow Valenti, Cartright and Judy were all tied in together, but the knot eluded him. He edged his speed up past the limit. Maybe the answer was in Palm Beach. If so the sooner he got there the quicker he would find it.

CHAPTER THREE

*D**eputy Sheriff Bill** Longworth* pushed aside some reports he had been studying and indicated a chair beside his desk. When Jeff was seated the man regarded him with quiet interest.

"How is Burrows?" he asked. The voice was soft and with a faint southern accent. "I haven't seen him for a long time. He drops me a note now and then but I never seem to have time to answer." A finger indicated the papers. "No one ever told me about the paperwork connected with this job. When I first took it I thought it was just cops and robbers stuff. You know. Bang! Bang! and down the highway with siren going. What can I do for you?"

As Longworth talked Jeff had been making his own appraisal. It was hard to tell the deputy's age. He was prematurely grey, of that he was certain. There were fine lines in his face but the years had not put them there. It was as though the wind and sun had drawn them. He had an odd smile. It started with a crinkle about clear, brightly inquisitive eyes and barely seemed to reach the lips. Jeff thought that he was probably a tough and dedicated cop, a relentless man, filled with an icy hatred for those he pursued. With a start he realized that the deputy was waiting for an answer to his question.

"I'm not sure that you can do anything. Theoretically I'm on a vacation, but Burrows has a bad memory. I've been staying down at a little place called Redemption Cay. Grant called and wanted me to check on a man by the name of Edward Valenti. He's supposed to be here."

Longworth shook out a cigarette, lit it and blew carefully on the match. His eyes never left Jeff's. Finally he snorted with wry admiration.

"That Burrows taps a lot of sources of information. Even the local papers don't know about Valenti and no one was going to tell them. It isn't the kind of publicity Palm Beach wants. The only reason I'm admitting it to you is that you'll probably track him down, since you know he's here. Besides, Grant did me a big favor once. I like to keep square with something like that."

"Where can I find him?"

"Why should anyone care?" There was a measured anger in the question. "A cheap thief. A murderer. A little man who started out with a big gun. A rat who pretended he was a tiger." The deputy rose. He was tall, lean, and as hard as a steel spring. There was a controlled fury in his stride as he paced across the room and then wheeled to confront Jeff, his eyes like glacial crystals. "I know he was top man. Big business. Two-hundred-and-fifty-dollar suits, penthouses, cars, dames—but he carried filth with him wherever he went. I hate the breed. Because of Valenti and what he controlled, men have killed each other. Kids went on the H and to get a fix they stole, lied, sold themselves and broke the hearts of their parents. Little people put money which should have gone for food and rent into the hands of his bookies. Still smaller people took their dimes and quarters and gave them to the policy runners. Why should any decent newspaper even want to print his name?"

Jeff thought he had never looked upon such implacable fury and then, suddenly, Longworth relaxed. The tension seemed to drain from him and he made an almost apologetic gesture.

"I get that way sometimes. It's a form of occupational cramps. Maybe I should be in some other work." He paused for a second and then, almost regretfully, continued. "Valenti, only he's not using that name, is aboard a forty-eight-foot cruiser up in Hobe Sound. That's a pretty exclusive section of the waterway; big homes along the shore, nice people. They won't like to hear about their neighbor even if he is only anchored out of the channel. I wish you'd leave it alone."

"I'll tell you what I'll do. If he is just there and I can't get anything really important out of him I'll leave it." Jeff grinned. "Valenti might turn out to be quite a tourist attraction. Have you thought about that?"

"The wrong kind of tourists for Palm Beach, the gapers and those who have a picnic on someone's lawn and think it's all right because they're tourists and, 'Hell, we're spendin' our good money in Florida, ain't we?' "

"Who owns the cruiser?"

"She's locally owned and up for charter during the winter months. The deal was made two weeks before Valenti was released. Jock McElroy, the owner and captain, got his first asking price but I don't guess he was surprised. There aren't many persons who can afford a boat and services like his and those who can don't usually quibble about money. Mostly his charters want to go down around the Keys, over to the Bahamas and the Out Islands. So far Valenti hasn't gone anyplace. Jock's proud of his boat. It must burn him just to sit there."

"Anything else?"

The deputy thrust a tongue against his cheek and the small lines of amusement were briefly etched about his eyes. Finally, he reached for the fawn-colored Stetson on his desk. "Fifteen minutes later and you would have missed me. I was on my way to call on Valenti. Come along and see for yourself."

They drove in an unmarked county car to the Municipal Dock and walked out to where an open-cockpit Chris-Craft was moored. A youth, shirtless and in oil-stained white duck trousers, made a burlesqued pretense of consternation.

"I'll swear I didn't do it, Sheriff," he pleaded.

Longworth shook his head sadly. "Charley always says it just that way and I always pretend it's the first time I've heard it." He turned to the boy. "I want to go up the Sound of the *Oriole II.*"

"Sure. Hop in, Sheriff. You know me. Always a man to be on the side of law and order."

They sat three abreast on the forward seat. Curtains of jeweled spray fanned out on either side of the bow as Charley fed in the gas and the motor drummed heavily. Jeff's eyes followed the lake's eastern shore with the undisguised interest of a tourist who looks upon the fabulous Palm Beach for the first time. West Palm Beach had seemed to be a lively, thriving city without any particular character to distinguish it from a thousand communities of similar size. But Palm Beach, what he could see of it in glimpses through the palms and at the ends of fine gardens, still retained the evidence of great wealth and an elegance that had made it internationally famous. He smiled at the idea that Valenti or his kind could intrude upon it. He wanted to ask Longworth about some of the homes so fleetingly seen but the roar of the motor made conversation impossible. Then, the sound died abruptly, the bow settled gently and he could feel the drag as though brakes were being applied. Charley was a good boatman. He edged his craft expertly alongside the cruiser.

There were four persons on the awninged afterdeck. Three men and a tall, beautifully proportioned blonde in white sharkskin shorts with a crimson bandeau drawn tightly across her breasts. She rose with a lazy, swinging, indolent interest and stood looking down at Jeff and Longworth.

"It's the law," she called over her shoulder with an amused inflection in her husky voice.

Standing in the Chris-Craft Jeff's eyes traveled from the girl to the men. One, despite the day's warmth, was covered from the waist down by a light, cashmere shawl. He was bare from the waist up. A monkey of a man. Perhaps he hadn't always been so, but now he seemed almost shriveled. The skin, stretched tightly over the balding skull and cheekbones, was prune-colored. Jeff made a quick guess at his height and thought he would measure about five feet six in the elevator shoes which he would undoubtedly wear. Now his lips moved and for a moment Jeff thought there had been no sound.

"Ask them aboard, Doris." The words were the faintest murmur.

The girl shrugged. "Hop on." She said indifferently. "Glad to have you aboard or whatever crap it is they say in the Navy." She contorted her full mouth in a leer. Jeff could find no other word for the expression. She winked, and it appeared obscene. "I used to hang around Sands Street and the Brooklyn Navy Yard."

"You talk too much, Doris." Again the whisper floated across the deck and it was the sound of dry reeds brushing together.

Jeff followed Longworth from the runabout to the cruiser's deck. The blonde surveyed them, her eyes traveling deliberately from their feet to their heads. Then she lifted one shoulder, as much as to say that she had seen better, and turned away.

Jeff looked at the other two men. They were clad in flowered Hawaiian shirts and sandals. One was a little too old for the crew cut he wore. He stared almost petulantly at the visitors. He was a big man with heavy shoulders, pillars of legs and big hands. A wrestler, maybe, or a pro football player no longer quite young enough for the game. The other man was lean to the point of being thin and where the shirt lay open the ribs were tight against his skin, which was tanned to a dark tobacco color that couldn't be acquired by a few weeks or even months in the Florida sun. He wore shell-rimmed glasses and behind the lenses the pupils of his eyes seemed unnaturally large. In his lap was a book he had been reading. He removed his glasses now and watched the strangers with an air of mild, scholarly reproof, as though they were boisterous intruders into a library. It was the man beneath the shawl, though, who held Jeff's attention. If Longworth knew what he was talking about this had to be Valenti.

"Doris—" a clawlike hand waved in the direction of the blonde— "said you were the law. I don't see a badge or a uniform but Doris, I think, has an instinct about such things. I am certain she would not make a mistake in such a matter." A thin smile held the lips briefly.

The blonde snorted and went to a table, mixing herself a drink. So this was Valenti, Jeff thought. He was puzzled by the diction and the choice of words. Valenti, he knew from what he had read, had little formal schooling. Somewhere along the way, or perhaps after he sat upon the heights, he had learned. Maybe it had been by imitation; it wouldn't have been difficult for a natural actor and mimic to acquire the patina of breeding and an easy fluency of speech which might pass for a measure of culture. It could be these very qualities which had lifted him from the muck of Delancey Street, set him apart from the young hoodlums.

This was the syndicate, the long hand reaching into a thousand hidden and profitable corners, the brain that had conceived Murder, Inc., and a multitude of interlocking gangs and individuals until they operated as a unit. It had made and unmade judges, mayors, police commissioners, district attorneys. Even in prison this brain had continued to direct the empire. Studying him now Jeff found it difficult to believe. The photographs he had looked at had been those of a slender, expressionless man who had seemed neither tall nor short. The years, though, had shrunk him. Valenti moved, sitting a little straighter in his chair, and Jeff realized that for all his appearance of frailty he was neither infirm nor helpless. Within him was an indomitable will, a power. It was something almost to be felt there upon the deck.

"What can I do for you?" The voice was stronger now and, oddly enough, almost challenging.

"You're Valenti?" Longworth's question was soft.

In the silence the tinkling of a spoon against glass as the blonde stirred her highball had the clear, sharp sound of wind bells.

The man seemed to consider the deputy's question, turning it over and eventually finding it reasonable. "I am *Mr.* Valenti," he said finally.

"We don't want you here, Valenti." Again Longworth's words were liquid.

"Who are *we?*" Valenti leaned slightly forward, interested.

"Let's put it this way. I don't want you here. Is that enough?"

"Why you big, dumb cop!" The blonde moved to confront them. The glass in her hand flew across the deck, missing Longworth but scattering part of its contents over his khaki shirt. "What the hell do you mean, coming here and talking that way? Why don't you be honest for once and just put out your hand?" She spoke to Valenti. "Give him the twenty-five bucks or whatever it is he came for and get rid of him. He's stinking up the joint." She was blazing with anger.

"Michael." Valenti's voice was weary. "Will you please take care of Doris?"

To Jeff's surprise it was the bespectacled one who rose. The muscle man, if there was one, should have been crew-cut boy. The one called Michael came quickly, so quickly that the girl only had time to retreat a few steps until her back touched the table. There was fear in her eyes and her fingers touched her mouth with a protective gesture. Michael's hand slapped her viciously across the face twice and then, what was more astonishing, he bent, swung her off the deck in his arms and casually tossed her over the rail and into the Sound. She fell with a wild yell, arms and legs flying, and disappeared with a heavy splash. When she came to the surface her face was all but hidden beneath wet and trailing hair. She clawed it away, spitting water and rage, treading water.

"You bastard!" The scream was venomous and shrill. "You God-damned skinny bastard. That's twice this week you've done that. It's going to make me sore if you keep it up."

Michael didn't even look her way. He went back to his chair, retrieved his book and replaced his spectacles. The one with the crew cut started to rise, stretching to see where the girl was swimming to the other side of the boat. Michael turned a page and spoke without lifting his eyes: "Sit down, Hallie!"

Crew Cut sat down as though he had been jolted. His mouth twitched and he began cracking the knuckles in his hands. Jeff couldn't resist winking at Longworth. It had been a surprising exhibition. Michael appeared as though he would have trouble wielding a fly swatter. Yet, when he had lifted the girl the muscles had flexed as though he had been strung upon steel cables. He had made the whole thing seem effortless.

"Doris unfortunately reverts now and then to her apprenticeship, when twenty-five dollars was the asking price." Valenti spoke conversationally, his eyes upon Longworth. "You were saying?" He was politely inquisitive.

"I was saying I don't want you here."

"And in what capacity do you speak, Mr.—?"

"I'm a deputy sheriff. My name's Longworth."

"And this gentleman?" Valenti nodded.

Jeff replied for himself. "My name's Martin. Jeff Martin. I'm a reporter from the New York *Globe*. I wanted to talk with you about your plans, why you are here, where you're going."

There was a sound and movement behind them. Doris came across the deck, dripping water, the shorts, beneath which she wore nothing, pressed tightly to her moulded loins. She glared at them as though they were to blame for everything.

"Cops!" The word was an indictment. "Lousy cops. Why don't you let people alone?" She turned and disappeared below, leaving a puddled trail.

"Why am I here?" Valenti shrugged. "Why shouldn't I be here? My plans? I have none except to cruise along the coast and lie in the sun."

"There ought to be more to it than that, part of a lifetime to be made up. I'd like an hour with you. There are a lot of unanswered questions, things which only you know and which could be told safely now." Jeff waited hopefully.

Valenti shook his head. "You're smart enough to know you don't make up lost years. Also, I have never liked newspapermen or answering questions." He dismissed Jeff without another word and turned his attention to Longworth. "I don't intend to stay here, but," and the words crackled electrically, "if I did want to stay in Palm Beach you wouldn't be able to stop me."

"I won't argue that." The deputy refused to be provoked. "But if you or your friends come ashore you'll be picked up."

"On what charge?" Valenti was again mildly interested.

"We can always find a charge." Longworth's eyes lighted and he smiled without restraint. "We'll find a charge, local or county. The books are filled with them. Keep out of Palm Beach, Valenti."

"*Mr.* Valenti!" The correction was a lash, no longer whispered.

"Have it your own way." Longworth turned away and spoke to Jeff. "Let's go."

They didn't speak again until they had walked back the length of the Municipal Dock and had reached the deputy's car. There Longworth lit a cigarette, leaned against a fender and stared musingly at the craft-dotted water as it sparkled in the late sunshine. Finally he sighed.

"I don't learn much." He admitted regretfully. "When I see a spider I want to step on it. I don't know a damn thing about spiders; maybe I should just watch it, see how it lives, what it feeds on and where the food comes from. I'd learn something. A dumb cop. Maybe she was right." He laughed without mirth or sound. "Where are you staying?" He snapped the cigarette away.

"I haven't checked in any place yet. I'll get my car and find a motel or go back to the Cay. It's a short run, and I didn't bring even a toothbrush."

"You can buy a toothbrush and I'll lend you a shirt if you want it. Come up to my place and spend the night." The invitation was made to sound casual but, somehow, Jeff thought he detected a note of loneliness in it. Longworth opened his door and slid behind the wheel. When Jeff was in he pulled away and into the traffic. "If I don't watch myself," Longworth continued, "I get antisocial. Maybe it's the job. You can get lonely at it. Anyhow, I've got plenty of room and it's not a bad place. Better than a motel. Well." He turned to Jeff with a small grin. "Better than those motels without swimming pools."

"Thanks." Jeff sensed he would be impatient with the conventional, polite demurrals.

"Good. I'll have someone pick up your car." He reached for the short-wave transmitter on the dash and told the office where he was and where he was going. Then he drove a few blocks in silence. "That blonde was a dish, wasn't she?" He made the statement with such bemused irrelevancy that Jeff laughed.

"I didn't see you even look at her. I guess you're mortal after all."

Longworth smiled shyly. "I relax right out of myself sometimes and usually with someone like that." He whistled tonelessly for a moment. "I guess you can't square that with what I said about the fringe element, can you?"

"I haven't tried."

"Girls like that one take an awful booting around. They start out all starry-eyed, and then little by little the stars disappear. Even a good dog will turn mean if it is kicked by everyone it meets. So what do you expect from a girl? It isn't her fault. The worst one like her expects is that she'll be laid and, probably, left. Who's to tell her that she's going to get her teeth knocked in? So what I said about Valenti and the two with him doesn't have to go for the dish. She's only one of the casualties I was talking about. She's one of the by-products of the system they set up." He was silent for half a block more. "I read a lot about this Valenti when I heard he was here." The statement was made abruptly.

From the corner of his eye Jeff tried to catch the other's expression. He understood that Longworth was smart enough to know he had briefed himself in exactly the same way. He wondered if the deputy was, also, running down an identical thread of speculation. He could be feeling him out. Well, there was no harm in that. For a second he was tempted to tell him about Senator Carter, of Judy, even, but he checked the impulse. Senator Carter was Judge Amos Cartright and not a felon. A man had a right to disappear if he wanted to. Cartright didn't fall within Longworth's field. He was a reporter's find, a sensational story, and Jeff would have had it on the wire by now if it weren't for the uneasy conviction that there was a tie-in between Valenti's being in Florida and Senator Carter of Redemption Cay. He wanted to join the links if they existed.

"How do you like Redemption Cay?" Longworth's voice almost startled him.

"I didn't think there was a place like it left in Florida."

"There isn't." Longworth pulled up before a two-storied, frame house and cut the motor. "Someone will come along and spoil it. It always happens. By the way, it's in my county, so I may drop in on you, unofficially."

Again Jeff wondered if, in the files of the Palm Beach papers, Longworth had stumbled across what he had found in Miami. He shook his head. It would be too much of a coincidence. Just the same this deputy was a man with a ranging imagination. Maybe a visit to Redemption Cay would be unofficial and maybe it wouldn't.

"This is it." Longworth moved out from behind the wheel and stood waiting until Jeff came around to join him. "Let's see if we can find a drink."

The deputy occupied the upper story of the structure. The living room was light, airy and immaculate. Outside, a balcony extended along two sides of the building, one section facing Lake Worth several blocks away. It was a two-bedroom apartment as orderly and as functional, Jeff thought, as the man who lived there. On one wall was a glass case enclosing a gun rack. There were a couple of shotguns, a high-powered rifle and a submachine gun.

"Are those loaded?"

Longworth smiled. "A gun that isn't loaded isn't any good. It's a club."

In the spotless kitchen the officer took out ice, glasses, a bottle of Scotch and one of bourbon. "How do you take it, and what?"

"Bourbon with a little water."

Longworth nodded approvingly. "That's a real good drink. I keep the Scotch for show. It's never been opened." He handed the bourbon to Jeff. "Pour your own."

Back in the breeze-swept living room again, while the deputy put in a call to someone at a garage asking that a boy be sent to the sheriff's office to pick up a car, Jeff stood by a bamboo table. On its top was a large album for photographs. Idly he turned back the cover and stiffened with surprise. Covering the page was a large photograph in color of an automobile wreck. Strewn on the road were mangled bodies, and the body of a girl hung halfway out of the crumpled front seat. The crimson-splashed victims seemed to leap from the picture with an almost terrifying impact. Curious now, he turned other pages. Here was murder, sudden death on the highway, the bullet-riddled body of a girl in a shabby room, a man sprawled awkwardly on the floor of a cheap bar, a Negro lying in the white sunlight with half his face cut away. Jeff sucked in his breath. In his time he had covered a lot of homicides and accidents, but this color process created an effect he wouldn't have believed possible. He became aware of the fact that Longworth was standing behind him and he turned questioningly.

"Gets you, doesn't it?"

Jeff whistled softly. "Right down where I live. Why?" He shook his head. "This is pretty grim stuff to have lying around to show visitors. It must make quite an impression."

They walked outside and took deck chairs on the veranda.

Not until they were settled did Longworth reply to the question. "For one thing, I don't have many visitors. The color process was an idea of mine. I tried to sell it to the county, but couldn't interest anyone. So I bought my own equipment, fitted up a darkroom where I could develop, print and enlarge what I took. You'd be surprised the effect one of those blown-up photographs has on a jury. In black and white it's just another accident or killing. In color they can see the blood and smell it. It's real. They're not just looking at a picture. They are there, part of what happened."

There was a quiet but intense enthusiasm in the deputy's voice; the first Jeff had detected since they met. Again he thought, This is a dedicated cop, a man with a single purpose; yet he was mild of manner and speech, a quietly pleasant companion.

"How did you get into this work? I still have a little trouble reconciling you with it. You don't look it, but I have an idea you're a tough man in a tangle."

Longworth stared out toward the water and across the crested palms. "I don't know," he confessed. "I don't mean about being tough. Those are only words. Sometimes you're tough because you have to be; it's a matter of self-preservation. A man is a fool to throw his weight around when it isn't necessary. It wears him out. About the work? Well." He took a long and reflective swallow of his drink. "I had four years at the university at Gainesville. When I graduated I started looking around for something to do. The army saved me the trouble. After the war I came out knowing a lot of things for which there didn't seem to be a market in civilian life. The sheriff of this county was a friend of my father's.

He offered me a job. It was just a job at first but then I began to get interested. I saw a lot of things and began to wonder why they happened. Then they sent me to Washington to take a course that the FBI gives. That was when I discovered it was, or could be, more than cops and robbers. That's about it."

"Do you like it? It hasn't become routine?"

Longworth chuckled quietly. "It sure isn't routine." He was thoughtful and then continued. "I must like it or I wouldn't stay. I used to wonder myself. If I just wanted to make myself feel important I could drive around the county and make half a dozen arrests a day on all sorts of violations. If I wanted to make money I could put the bite on the cat houses in town, the dice games, the little hustlers in small hotels. If I wanted security I'd go into Civil Service. The sheriff's office is elective, so you get a new sheriff and maybe he appoints new deputies. I could be out of a job at the next election." He shook his head and gave a small, almost embarrassed laugh. "How the hell did we get into this?"

"I've always been curious. I've known good and bad police officers but in the beginning they all must have had something in common. Is it a passion for order?"

"Maybe that's it. The majority of people are decent, law-abiding, wanting to put down roots and willing to grind away at the same old job day after day. But along the edges are the frustrated and the envious. They're the guys on the prowl, and the honest man is unable to protect himself against them because his mind doesn't work as theirs do. Someone has to give him a hand. Why it has to be me or men like me I honestly don't know." He finished his drink and held the empty glass in his hand. "How long are you going to be in Florida?"

"I'm not sure. Burrows wanted a story on Valenti. I still don't have it and probably won't get it, but Grant is a pretty reasonable man, for a city editor. If someone won't talk you can't make him. I could hop this up with a short lead on Valenti being here aboard a cruiser with a blonde and then fill it out with background. It might fool the readers into thinking they were getting something hot and fresh, but it wouldn't fool Grant. That's why I'm not going to try."

Longworth, who had been staring out at the water, grunted and rose abruptly. He went inside and reappeared almost immediately with a pair of binoculars. He stood, fixing them on an object. Then he turned and handed the glasses to Jeff.

"Valenti." He jerked his head in the direction of Lake Worth.

Jeff adjusted the binoculars to his own eyes and swept them across the stretch of water, holding when he came to the cruiser. As she made a turn, the stern came into view and he could see the name: *Oriole II. W. Palm Beach, Fla.* There was only one figure on the afterdeck now. It was Valenti. As Jeff watched, a white-coated steward approached the chair, apparently asked a question, bent down for the answer, nodded and disappeared. Jeff lowered the glasses.

"You must have scared him off."

Longworth shook his head as he lit a cigarette. "He doesn't scare." He saw the unasked question on Jeff's face. "Oh, I meant what I said and he knew it, but it wouldn't scare him. He wouldn't hightail it because a sheriff's deputy said scat. No." He shook his head. "He's going wherever he's going because that is what he had planned." He hesitated, "I've got a hunch that maybe this isn't just a pleasure trip after all. I sure can't tell you why." He took the binoculars from Jeff's outstretched hand and wrapped the strap about them. "How about having a couple more drinks and then we'll go out and eat? I know a great place for fried shrimp and cold beer if that appeals to you."

"That appeals to me fine." Jeff stood up and stretched luxuriously.

With his eyes on the channel marker, Jock McElroy was taking the *Oriole II* southward. This was the damnedest charter he could ever remember having. Anchored like a scow for two weeks and then off with five minutes' notice. Instead of going outside, as he had wanted, they were following the inland waterway. The *Oriole II* was too good a boat for that. She could go any place, almost. Ordinarily Jock could have predicted what would have happened after he first set eyes on that long-legged blonde. A couple more girls should have come aboard. There would be a lot of drinking and sliding in and out of bed. The radio would be going day and night and there would be some fights to liven things up. Cold beer in the mornings for hangovers and the drinking starting again before lunch. But it hadn't turned out that way. He couldn't figure them out. They didn't want to fish, they didn't get drunk, and the radio went on only a couple of times a day for the news.

He leaned against the wheel. This was damned monotonous. What's more, the girl didn't seem to belong to anyone. The big fellow with the short hair followed her around with his eyes all the time but Jock had never seen him try and make a pass. The other didn't do anything but read all the time and the old man, wrapped up like a mummy, wanted to lie in the sun. There was something about the old man. Sometimes it was hard to hear what he said. But, by God, the others heard and jumped when he spoke. It was good money and a three-month charter but, privately, he didn't think much of their manners. To hell with it, he decided. If they laid over in Miami, he'd get laid ....

Doris listlessly drew a card, frowned over what she should throw away and then tossed the entire hand on the table with a snort of exasperation.

"Why do we have to stay on this damn boat?" She demanded. "Why can't we go to a hotel at Miami and live like everyone else, with something to do?"

"Pick up your hand, Doris." Valenti spoke quietly.

"I don't want to play any more gin. I'm getting a callous on my fingers from these damn cards. I'm supposed to be having fun." She was momentarily defiant.

"You're supposed to do what I tell you to do." Valenti lifted his eyes and stared at her.

Beneath the cold glare Doris shivered and her confidence vanished. Her lips trembled involuntarily and her hands gathered up the scattered cards.

"Well. I—I don't know why you brought me along," she protested weakly.

"I brought you along because you are a pretty girl. It has been a long time since I have seen one. It gives me pleasure to look at you, to smell your perfume, to watch you walk."

"But—" she was honestly confused—"you don't do anything about it. No one tries to do a damn thing about it; not even that big oaf over there." She jerked her head scornfully to where the man with the crew cut sat. "My God! If he isn't good for that what *is* he good for? It mixes a girl all up. You'd think I was a eunuch or something!"

Valenti permitted a wisp of a smile to flit across his face. "That would surprise me, Doris. That would surprise me very much." He half turned in his chair. "Hal. Get me a little sherry."

The big man hurriedly laid aside the comic book he was reading and went to a buffet, filling a slender glass with pale sherry. He brought it quickly and stood waiting.

"That's all, Hal."

"Yeah. Sure. Thanks, boss." He almost stumbled in his haste to reseat himself and fell into the chair as though he had been running and was exhausted.

"Yeah. Sure. Thanks, boss," Doris mimicked him, and her eyes were filled with contempt. "My God! You'd think someone had come at you with a whip."

"Play your cards, Doris." Valenti sipped his sherry.

Angrily she put down a ten of diamonds.

"Gin." Valenti took the card and spread his hand. Then he leaned back in his chair and studied her pensively. "You're smarter than I thought, Doris. It's impossible that, even with a brain like yours, you didn't know that the ten would gin me. It was a way of ending the game. I like that." He pushed his chair back from the table. "Come here." When she was at his side he drew her into his lap.

She settled gingerly. "Jesus," she said. "I'm always afraid I'm going to break you in two."

Valenti spat in her face. One hand moved, snake-like, to her throat and the fingers wound about it as a prehensile claw. Her scream was cut off but her mouth remained open and her eyes were wide, staring and terror-filled. The sound which came from between her parted lips was bubbling and strangled. In her fear and pain she writhed and twisted frantically but Valenti's other hand, clamped to her wrist, held her.

"Don't you ever say a thing like that again. Do you understand? Do you understand?" He shook her, his own body trembling with fury. Then he relaxed the pressure of the fingers at her throat, releasing her, and she slid from his inclined legs to the floor. She stared up at him, stricken. One hand moved about her throat, soothing it. Her eyes never left his face.

"You must remember who and what you are, Doris." He spoke calmly. "If you don't forget that we will get along very well. If you forget it I will kill you."

She nodded dumbly and the tips of her fingers tried to wipe away the spittle. Valenti tossed a handkerchief down to her.

"Clean your face and come back here."

She came obediently, cowed. Her movement was almost furtive as she fearfully reseated herself on his lap. Valenti nodded amiably as though he had no recollection of the incident. It was something that had never happened. His fingers moved down the buttons of her blouse, unfastening it until it lay open, and his hand traveled over her body, playing, pinching, smoothing and caressing. She offered no response but submitted stolidly.

"I am usually well pleased with you, Doris." The words were a trifle husky. "If you pretended too much, I would know that you were just a beautiful cow with big breasts. But there are things to keep in mind. Don't pretend too much, but don't presume."

"I don't know why you talk to me that way." The words were barely audible.

"Because it makes me feel good." A curious note of exultation crept into the voice. "I've had a lot of years when I didn't know what it was to feel good." The searching fingers pulled away the brassiere and then stripped the blouse from her shoulders until she sat exposed, classically beautiful. Hal stared over the top of his comic book with covert hunger and agony. "Now, I feel good again. I begin to feel like the man I was."

Michael entered the saloon. His eyes flicked over the scene and then he ignored it. He could have been alone in the cabin as he went to the buffet and made himself a drink. He stood with his back to the others but when he had tested the highball and found it to his liking he selected a chair by a table. He turned on the lamp and picked up a book.

Doris moved a little uncomfortably. What was happening wasn't particularly important in itself. She knew she was beautiful and being put on display this way appealed to her vanity. What bothered her was the fact that it seemed to be making so little impression. For the first time a trace of coyness manifested itself. She inclined her blonde head, her lips touching Valenti's ear.

"Why don't we go to the cabin, honey?" She whispered the words but not so softly that the others could not hear.

With the heel of one hand Valenti pushed her head back and away. "You are a cow, Doris. Beautiful, but a cow. It's too bad."

The full, ripe mouth pouted sulkily and then some latent appreciation for the ridiculous asserted itself. With an assumption of nonchalance she stretched across Valenti to the table, took a cigarette from a box, lit it and blew a fine, thin stream from between her teeth.

She laughed. "All I can say is that this is one hell of a boat ride."

Valenti patted her shoulder approvingly. "Hal!" He ordered. "Get me another glass of sherry, and I would like a cigar before we eat. Doris, would you like something?"

"Hell yes. Let's booze it up." She rose and, indifferent to her semi-nakedness, strolled to the buffet and poured a pony of brandy. "Let's live, kids." She turned on the radio and a dance band's music filled the cabin. Michael glanced at her, annoyed. "To hell with you, Joe!" She tossed off the brandy. "Want to dance with me?" She moved provocatively in front of him. He pursed his lips and turned his attention to the book. She poured herself a second drink and returned to Valenti's lap. "We've really got it made, huh? Naked women, yachts, Florida sunshine."

"I am very pleased with you, Doris. Hal!" He put the cigar in his mouth and waited for a light. When the man came forward with a match Valenti inclined his head, forcing the big man to bend until his shaking hand was touching Doris's breast. She laughed, thrusting back her shoulders, pushing it closer.

"Where did you find him, in a zoo?" She leaned against Valenti. "He'd make a great mate for a gorilla."

"Hal has his uses." Valenti was reproving.

"Like what?" She scoffed.

"Like breaking your pretty neck in case I should want it done."

CHAPTER FOUR

S outhbound, the streamliner raced as a streak of mercury across the Florida coastal flatlands. In the observation car passengers sat over their drinks, reading, talking or staring out of the windows at the clustered pines and moss-draped, twisted oaks.

Near the center of the car a dapper little man in a neat, double-breasted suit of pin-striped flannel, was leafing through a magazine. He sipped almost daintily now and then from a tall, frosted glass of lemonade. The tips of his glossily polished shoes just reached the carpet and he made small dancing movements with them as though they were marionettes activated by unseen strings.

The girl beside him, in a beautifully tailored suit of grey silk, with a small knot of fresh violets pinned at the lapel, glanced and smiled. The man, catching her expression, smiled back. He was humming a tuneless sound, maintaining the rhythm of the clacking rails beneath speeding wheels.

"Can you do that on lemonade alone or do you spike it on the sly with gin?" Her voice was low and throaty.

"Oh! My, no." He seemed to be startled by the question. "I just feel good. You see"— he put the magazine aside— "this is my first vacation in years. I've been looking forward to it for so long. Florida!" He breathed the word ecstatically. "Do you know I've never been to Florida? Seems impossible, doesn't it, in this day when people move back and forth across the world so casually?" He removed a pince-nez, wiped the lenses with a crisp, white handkerchief and resettled them in place. "My name's Hathaway. Roland Hathaway." He made the admission diffidently. "I suppose it's all right to introduce myself this way." He was embarrassed. "You mustn't think I am trying to—to flirt with you, particularly since" — he looked around the crowded car—"well, since we are so very well chaperoned?"

She didn't laugh. Her smile was gentle. "No. I don't think you are trying to pick me—flirt. My name's Marcia Lewis."

"That's a pretty name. Marcia." He savored it. He hesitated uncertainly. "Would it be forward if I offered you some refreshment, Miss Lewis?" He hurried the invitation, stammering over it.

"Thank you." She smiled again.

Pleased, he touched the bell with a carefully manicured finger and then turned to her with a grave concern. "You mustn't think I disapprove of liquor, Miss Lewis." He flushed. "What I mean to say is that because I am taking lemonade don't think you must have something nonalcoholic."

"It hadn't occurred to me, Mr. Hathaway." Her expression was grave, but there were small lights of amusement behind her eyes. When the waiter came she ordered Scotch and soda. Mr. Hathaway beamed.

"I believe people should do the things they want to do." He bent toward her with a conspiratorial air. "I'll confess something. All my life I have wondered what a sherry cobbler was. One of these days I am going to walk right into a saloon and order it." He nodded emphatically.

She placed the highball on a coaster and took a silver case from her purse. Mr. Hathaway watched with pleased interest as she lit a cigarette and inhaled deeply.

"You do that so gracefully, Miss Lewis." The compliment was sincere. "Young people these days are all so graceful, so really beautiful. I mean that honestly. It isn't— what is the slang expression?"

"A line?" She laughed and the sound was a fresh, bubbling spring within her throat.

"Yes. Of course. A line. Do you know, I have always been puzzled about exactly what it means?"

"To catch fish you use a line. I suppose that is what it means." She leaned back in the chair, slender legs neatly crossed at the ankles, and regarded him with a faintly speculative consideration.

"Oh! Of course." Mr. Hathaway seemed put out with himself for not thinking of this obvious explanation. "When one goes fishing one uses a line. It is not at all abstruse when you think of it that way. Not at all abstruse." He was grateful. "Whenever I hear that expression I shall remember you, Miss Lewis."

With a lazy, easy movement she leaned forward and picked up her glass, taking a thoughtful swallow and touching one of the ice cubes with the tip of her tongue.

"Where are you going in Florida, Mr. Hathaway?"

"I'm not really sure. I'm just being a vagabond, a gypsy. I suppose that sooner or later everyone gets to Miami, so I'll have to go there. But I really want to see Palm Beach. I think I've heard of Palm Beach for as long as I can remember. It's quite fashionable. Years ago—and I'm sure I don't know why I should know this—there was a very famous gambling casino there. Bradley's, I believe." He made the statement as though it were indelicate. "I don't imagine it is in existence now but I certainly would have liked to have seen it in its day. I'll go to Palm Beach first. After that I thought I might take one of those Greyhound buses and go adventuring." He halted abruptly. "You mustn't think I am too naïve, Miss Lewis. It is just that I have been planning this trip for years and now that it is here, well, honestly, I'm excited as a child on Christmas morning. I suppose it is foolish."

"I don't think so at all." She was sympathetic. "I'm tired of these people who are bored with life. You're refreshing, Mr. Hathaway."

"That's very kind, very kind indeed. I was afraid I might be wearying you. By the way, if it isn't being presumptuous, where are you going, Miss Lewis?"

She hesitated briefly and then her smile was softly radiant. "By a coincidence I am, also, going to Palm Beach. I have friends there."

"How nice. How very nice." He was delighted, and then his expression became wistful. "I suppose— I suppose it would be too much to expect we might meet again? It isn't a large place, or so I understand."

"Who knows?" She touched his wrist with her fingers. "As you say, it isn't a very large city."

"Well, then, we shall leave it to the goddess of chance." He stood up and smoothed his coat. "If you'll excuse me now, I have some last-minute things to put in my bags."

She nodded and her gaze followed him as he moved down the length of the car, swaying slightly with the train's motion. There was a rushing sound as he opened the vestibule door out of her line of vision and then the only intrusive note was the muted clatter of wheels upon rails. She lit a second cigarette, slowly, pre-occupied and faintly puzzled. Finally she turned and her finger found the wall bell. The steward came and stood before her.

"Do we make a stop before Palm Beach?"

"Yes'm."

"Then I'd like to send a telegram."

She went to a desk in the corner of the car, took a pad of yellow blanks from the rack, and, after momentary hesitation, began to write. Finished, she read the wire over carefully and signaled the waiter, giving it to him with a five-dollar bill.

"Pay for it and keep the change but be sure it gets off."

"Yes'm. I sure will."

She remained at the desk, staring unseeingly out the window, tapping her teeth meditatively with the end of the pen.

Mr. Hathaway unlocked his compartment on the through car from New York that had been attached to the streamliner at Jacksonville. His two bags were on the floor, packed and locked.

A current novel, which he had not finished, lay upon the seat. He lifted one of the bags, placed it on the divan and opened it. His clothing was as meticulously packed as he was dressed.

He weighed the novel in his hand and finally tucked it in an inside flap of the suitcase. Then Mr. Hathaway did a surprising thing.

He lifted the carefully ordered shirts at one end of the bag and withdrew a 38-caliber revolver. His thumb slid the catch and he flipped the cylinder out, taking a quick glance at the filled chambers before he snapped it back into place. Then he carefully put the gun away beneath the shirts, closed the bag's lid and locked it.

He settled himself on one end of the divan near the window and his fingernails made small, nicking sounds as he allowed them to play along the sill. He experienced a creeping sensation of excitement. After all this time, the years of persistent determination, long after everyone else had written it off, things were beginning to move. Sooner or later they must fall into place. It was a mathematical certainty. Patience was a virtue Mr. Hathaway cultivated assiduously.

The chief of police of West Palm Beach leaned back in his chair and regarded Mr. Hathaway with frank astonishment. Then he picked up the telephone and made a call to the sheriff's office. While he waited for the connection his eyes never left Mr. Hathaway's face. He shook his head incredulously and then spoke in reply to a voice at the other end of the wire.

"Let me have Deputy Longworth." He held the receiver slightly away from his ear. "Bill? This is Johnson. Have you got a minute or two? I'd like to have you come over. Fine!" He replaced the instrument in its cradle and lit a cigar. Mr. Hathaway was cherubic as he nodded approvingly. He was humming softly to himself.

"I suppose you know what you're talking about?" The officer was still doubtful.

"Oh! My. Yes." Mr. Hathaway was emphatic. "It has to be here. I mean, it has to be in Florida. The whole thing would be too fortuitous otherwise. This movement isn't an accident. Nothing that occurs from now on will be other than part of the design. We must remember with whom we deal. If Mr. Valenti wanted a rest, a period of recuperation, he would simply have rented a house or gone to a hotel. Mr. Valenti is unfamiliar with boats, so he doesn't like them. I mean that as a generalization, you understand. Persons of Mr. Valenti's, shall we say, background, don't charter a boat for an extended cruise. The life aboard a boat would be alien to them. Mr. Valenti and his companions would be much more at home in one of the large hotels in Miami."

The chief nodded, partly satisfied. "You may have something there. It would figure."

"I'm certain of it." Mr. Hathaway tapped the fingertips of both hands together. He was as chipper as a sparrow on a wire. "We must consider the presence of Miss Marcia Lewis, who isn't Miss Marcia Lewis at all but Mrs. Dale Blake, formerly Dale Harper. Miss Harper, Mrs. Blake or Miss Lewis—whichever you prefer, it really doesn't make any difference—has led a most casual life, most casual indeed, though you would never suspect it from looking at her. She is a charming and cultivated young woman of considerable physical beauty. She had some minor success in pictures, I believe, and then, for reasons best known to herself, married Harry Blake in Hollywood. This Mr. Blake came to a speedy and untimely end. He was unfortunate enough to be sitting in front of an open window on a warm night when someone decided to shoot through it." He uttered a clucking sound of disapproval.

"I still don't get the tie-in." Johnson rolled the cigar between his fingers. "Valenti, yes. The girl? Where does she come into the picture?"

Mr. Hathaway chortled. "What you don't know is that our Mrs. Blake, née Harper, is the sister of James Harper, who was convicted and still serves a sentence in jail. She was about ten years old when he was sent away but as she grew older she visited him when permitted. A shocking experience for a young girl, to see her brother in jail. They have, of course, corresponded, and Harper has undoubtedly sent her messages through other inmates who have been released. Oh, make no mistake about this. Miss Marcia Lewis knows exactly what she is doing."

The door opened and Bill Longworth entered. He glanced at Mr. Hathaway, who had turned in his chair at the sound, and then at Chief Johnson.

"How are you, Tom?"

Johnson indicated Mr. Hathaway with his cigar and then leaned back almost expectantly. "Meet Mr. Hathaway, Bill. Deputy Sheriff Longworth, Mr. Hathaway."

"I'm delighted to know you." Mr. Hathaway regarded Longworth happily over the joined tips of his fingers.

"I asked Bill to come over." Johnson explained. "Because he has already had some contact with your man."

Bill darted a quick, inquiring glance at the police chief. There was a small grin on the officer's face. He pushed a box of cigars across the desk. The deputy shook his head.

"Mr. Hathaway is looking for Edward Valenti, Bill." He offered the information as though it were part of a joke.

"Well, not exactly." Mr. Hathaway was precise. "I'm looking for something over a million dollars. Mr. Valenti is incidental."

Johnson chuckled quietly at the expression of bewilderment on Longworth's face.

"Mr. Hathaway," he explained, "is an investigator for Zenith Indemnity, the company that carried the insurance on that armored car holdup in Brooklyn years ago. He thinks Valenti has the money."

"Tch-tch-tch!" Mr. Hathaway was patently annoyed by such a loose summation of the case. "That isn't at all the situation, gentlemen. I don't think Valenti has it. As a matter of fact I know he hasn't. I believe, however, he is looking for it." He sighed unhappily.

Bill Longworth felt a quick tingle of excitement and a galvanizing interest. The hunch had been right after all. "How did the money get to Florida?"

"Someone brought it, naturally." Mr. Hathaway was pedantic.

"Who and when?" The deputy leaned forward in his chair, staring intently at the investigator.

Mr. Hathaway was lecturing a dull student. "If I knew who," he spoke distinctly, "the money would have been recovered long ago. As to when, I have no way of determining that. But I should say that it was after the trial and conviction of those involved. They were all very sure they would get off. Influence had moved up into the district attorney's office and, I am quite certain, even to the bench itself."

"Well, now, Mr. Hathaway." Johnson was dubious. "You just don't give over a million dollars to someone and say 'Hold this for me until I get back.'"

"However, that is exactly what happened." Mr. Hathaway emitted a sound of exasperation. "This case has been an irritation to me. There are so many obscure facets. Many, many obscure facets and dead ends."

He took a deep breath and expelled it between his teeth, his eyes roving from Johnson to Longworth.

"Now." He was crisp and began ticking off his points by tapping one finger after another. "We must assume that whoever was entrusted with the money has been delinquent; otherwise it would have been delivered to Mr. Valenti and there would be no necessity for him to come to Florida. So the thieves have fallen out and there is skulduggery afoot. Second, the area of search from a boat is limited. One may go ashore at a variety of places but one does not penetrate inland. From that we have to conclude that the knavish trustee of this money is somewhere on Florida's east coast or on one of the many remote hideaways in the waters between here and Key West. Third, it is quite obvious Mr. Valenti possesses only the most general information; otherwise he would have gone directly to the place. It is hearsay, rumor or fragmentary intelligence which he has gathered from those who shuttled in and out of prison while he was incarcerated. Fourth, we cannot ignore the presence of Miss Marcia Lewis. I will explain her to you later, Mr. Longworth."

Bill nodded. This was a terrier of a man, he thought, who would never give up but would worry and worry at the problem until he had torn it apart.

"We shall call Miss Lewis by that name to avoid confusion." Mr. Hathaway continued. "There is little reason to doubt that her brother has furnished her with such information as was passed along the grapevine. That, also, must be of a general nature only unless Mr. Valenti is completely baffled and the money is somewhere here in Palm Beach." He smiled comfortably, satisfied with the recapitulation.

"Wasn't there a record of the serial numbers on the large bills?" Longworth was intensely interested and Mr. Hathaway no longer seemed a slightly ludicrous figure. For all his size he became impressive as he talked.

"My goodness, yes! A few of them showed up after the robbery but then the trickle dried abruptly. The numbers, however, would present no insurmountable problem to Mr. Valenti at this time. Despite the fact that he has been in prison for many years and much of his evil empire has fallen apart, he is not completely shorn. It is true he no longer commands the full authority that was once his but he still has connections. He has connections in many parts of the world. Mexico. Italy. South America. Switzerland. Belgium. I may say, also, that despite his reputed wealth, this million or so dollars is no small sum to him, and he has no intention of letting it go. The bills could be exchanged simultaneously in half a dozen different countries and we would never be able to trace them fast enough to apprehend the culprits." He smiled gently, as though savoring a secret irony. "No, the serial numbers would present no great problem to Mr. Valenti. However, I think he will find there are other complications he hasn't foreseen ..."

"What about the FBI?" Johnson interposed. He, also, no longer smiled at Mr. Hathaway's mannerisms or speech.

"The FBI is naturally following Mr. Valenti's movements with considerable interest. You must understand, though, that this is an extremely personal issue with me. I have been annoyed by this case for many years. Once, I even had to take a sleeping tablet. It left me quite unnerved." He compressed his lips distastefully at the memory.

"I'm not sure exactly what we can do to help you, Mr. Hathaway." Longworth made the admission regretfully. "Valenti is out of either county or local jurisdiction."

"My goodness! I don't want any help, although it is kind of you to volunteer. I came merely to introduce myself and to determine whether the authorities knew of Mr. Valenti's whereabouts."

"The boat he chartered, *Oriole II,* took off yesterday." Longworth spoke regretfully.

"Well, if he has left I will simply have to follow him." He regarded Longworth sympathetically. "You musn't feel too bad about it. Fortunately, it isn't really complicated. From what Mr. Johnson told me, a boat the size of the one Mr. Valenti has chartered doesn't move about completely unnoticed. Sooner or later I shall locate it"— he patted his knees with both hands— "then I shall merely stay with Mr. Valenti until he locates what we both seek."

"These are very rough characters, Mr. Hathaway." Longworth gazed unhappily at the investigator. He was a nice little man, he mused, determined and angry. But Bill wondered if this would be enough in the big squeeze. "Do you think you can handle it? If the FBI is on it why not string along with them?"

Mr. Hathaway shook his head vigorously. "I am well aware of the unsavory nature of Mr. Valenti and his companions.

They are, indeed, reprehensible persons. However, I shall deal with them firmly when the time comes. Very firmly, you may be sure of that." The slender figure stiffened belligerently in the chair. Mr. Hathaway removed his glasses and polished them energetically.

"What about this Lewis girl?" The police chief laid his cigar carefully on the edge of a tray. "If it will help I can put a man on her while she's in town."

Mr. Hathaway shook his head. "That is exceedingly kind of you, Mr. Johnson. Unfortunately, I don't think Miss Lewis knows any more than I do. It would be too easy to expect her to lead us to the money. No. Miss Lewis must, also, ride in Mr. Valenti's wake, to adopt a metaphor." He smiled ingenuously. "Despite the seriousness with which I view this case the spectacle of thieves chasing thieves titillates me. Yes, indeed, it titillates me. Well." He almost bounced from the chair. "Thank you for your patience and courtesy. I think I will take a brisk walk. I have found it frequently helps in a situation of this sort." He went quickly to the door, closing it behind him.

Longworth turned a bemused attention upon the police chief. The man was staring at the blank wall as though he didn't believe what he had seen.

"Now." Johnson sighed gustily. "That is a real nice, little man. I sure would hate to see him get hurt. A thing like that would upset me. It sure would."

"Do you know something, Tom?" Longworth was thoughtful. "I think he is about the biggest little man I've ever seen. I think if I was on the other side I'd hate to cross him."

"Well." Johnson picked up his cigar and relit it carefully. "I guess he knows what he's doing. Anyhow, we've got our own troubles." He relaxed comfortably. "How's business?"

Longworth slid out of his chair. "We're getting by." He grinned. "Making expenses." His expression sobered. "I can't help it." The confession was made with wry humor. "I'd like to be dealt a hand in this just to see what I could draw."

"Take it easy and you'll live longer." Johnson was unenthusiastic. "Let everyone handle his own grief. I've got mine. Ronnie Tatum was killed last night on the highway trying to tag a drunk who was doing eighty-five miles an hour. The car sideswiped his motorcycle. It's too damn bad. He was a good man and with a wife and a couple of kids."

"I got the report. I'm sorry." Longworth hesitated. "Well, so long."

Johnson nodded without replying and began shuffling through some papers on his desk.

Standing before the open windows, looking out over the bright expanse of Lake Worth and to the sea beyond, Marcia Lewis turned expectantly in response to a knock at her door.

"Come in."

The man who entered was deceptively youthful in appearance. Only his eyes betrayed him. They were old, without luster. He wore a bright sport shirt loose outside his trousers and there were heavy, Mexican huaraches on his feet. He shut the door and stood with his back against it.

"Well?" There was a note of impatience in her voice.

"Cop!" The word came flatly.

"How do you know?"

His smile was almost patronizing. He lit a cigarette, drawing upon it heavily.

"I said, how do you know?" The question was snapped.

"When I got your wire I went down to the depot."

"I saw you there." She was keyed up. "Get on with it."

"Well." He was being exasperating deliberately. "I tailed him. Real gangster talk, huh?" He laughed, amused by his wit. "Anyhow, he went to the bus terminal first and checked his bags.

The next stop was the police station. He was in there about half an hour. A deputy sheriff came over but I don't know if there was any connection. It could be he had other business there. But you can lay big odds this one is a cop."

"What kind of cop?" She walked to a bureau and examined herself in the mirror above it.

"Who knows? He's sure not local, so maybe he's federal. What other kind of cop would be on it?" He flopped wearily down on the bed, bunching the pillows behind his head.

"Get up." The command was sharp. "When I want you in or on my bed I'll let you know."

He regarded her with a sleepy, faintly ironical smile but as she continued to stare at him he moved uneasily, yawned with pretended indifference and finally got up, trying to act as though it were his idea.

"Are you going to be hard to get along with, baby?"

"Where's Valenti?" She ignored his question.

"How do I know? On a boat someplace, heading south."

"You let him get away." There was bitter accusation in the words.

"What was I supposed to do, swim after him? When you telephoned from New York you said for me to meet you here. Well, I'm here. Is it my fault Valenti isn't? What do you want to do?"

"Look for him!"

"How?" He was being supercilious. "You going to get a water spaniel to track him down?"

"I don't know." She was indifferent to the sarcasm.

"It's going to get kind of crowded, isn't it? You, me, this cop Hathaway, and who knows who else. The word is out and the thieves will be pouring into Florida like it was a convention, all looking for Valenti and the loot."

She tapped her foot. "Who's with him?"

"A real punchy goon by the name of Hal Booker, Michael Spain, and a long-legged blonde. They were here, all except the blonde, ten days before Valenti was told to take the walk. How about a drink?"

She went to the telephone and he watched her with narrowed eyes.

"I'm checking out, operator. Will you send a boy up for my bags? Thank you."

"Hey!" The man protested. "You just got here. I haven't seen you in a long time. You act like it was some kind of a marathon race. Let's take it easy and have a little fun."

"By fun I suppose you mean crawling into the hay. Is that all you ever think of?"

"Tell me something better." He moved to her, his hands clasping her waist, drawing her into him.

"Later, Donnie. Later." She was annoyed.

He pushed her away roughly. "You're real chilly, aren't you? What is it? Someone else?"

"No." She spoke wearily. "I don't have anyone else. Does there have to be someone else or couldn't I just not be in the mood?"

"Maybe when you get in the mood I won't be." He was sulky.

She laughed and touched his cheek lightly. "Like a goat you won't be. Where's your car?"

"In a parking lot."

"We're going to Miami. You can pick up some clothes at your place. I'm not sure how these things work but I know a boat has to put in for gas some time. Maybe the Coast Guard keeps track of them. I don't know. We can ask, saying we were supposed to join a party aboard. When did he leave?"

"Yesterday afternoon." He tilted his head to one side and regarded her skeptically. "I still don't know what you're going to do when you catch up with Valenti."

"We'll have a talk. Part of that money is Jim's. I'll collect it for him."

He snorted. "That's what you think. Besides, your brother doesn't have any use for money while he's still in the trap. Besides that, Valenti isn't going to cut it up just because you ask."

"Valenti will play it right. He always has, Jim says."

"You're crazy. Real gone and crazy. Get in Valenti's way and all he'll do is give the word to Spain and that will be the end of you. Me too, if I'm fool enough to tag along."

"You can stay. I don't need you."

"I'll go. You know that." He was resigned. He lit a cigarette and drew upon it thoughtfully. "But it sounds like a pretty silly frolic to me. Valenti, from what you said, isn't sure where he's going. We don't know where we're going. Now. How in hell can you make a dime that way?"

There was a knock on the door and she made a motion of silence.

"Come in."

"You have some bags to go, Miss?" The boy looked around the room.

"Those two." She indicated the unopened luggage. "I'll meet you in the lobby."

She waited until the boy had left. "This is the way it figures, Donnie. All Jim could tell me is that Valenti knows who has it but he doesn't know exactly where he is. It was someone Valenti trusted, or thought he could. The thief blows a long time ago and all Valenti hears while he is in the trap is that he's down here, somewhere in Florida. I know as much as Valenti, except who we're looking for."

The man's laugh was mirthless. "That kind of gives him the edge, I'd say."

"That's why I want to talk with Valenti. When I do we'll know where we stand." She moved toward the door. "Now, let's go."

Mr. Hathaway purchased a package of mints from the girl at the cigar counter and while he forced out one with a fingernail his innocent gaze was upon her as she stopped at the cashier's window to pay her bill. He was preoccupied with the mints until he was certain she was crossing the lobby. Then he glanced up and smiled with delighted surprise.

"Well, Miss Lewis! As we said, Palm Beach isn't so large after all, is it?"

"Hello, Mr. Hathaway." For a moment she was uncertain and then the warm glow of her smile enveloped him. "How nice to see you again so soon. Are you enjoying yourself? Oh!" She made a quick gesture of apology. "This is my—my cousin Donald. Donald Trask. Mr. Hathaway."

"How do you do, Mr. Trask." Mr. Hathaway shook Donnie's limp hand. "May I compliment you on your choice of relatives?"

"Hi!" Donnie regarded Mr. Hathaway distastefully.

"Well!" She was bright, interested. "Is Palm Beach everything you thought it would be, Mr. Hathaway?"

"Confidentially, no, Miss Lewis." He lowered his voice. "I must confess I'm disappointed, although I suppose it's my own fault. You see, I had some romantic ideas about Palm Beach. Years ago, long before your time, Charles Dana Gibson, the artist, drew some scenes of Palm Beach. It must have been quite elegant. I remember the pen-and-ink sketches. Mr. Gibson made it very glamorous, with boys pedaling wicker chairs in which there were romantic-appearing men and quite handsome girls, shading their complexions from the sun with tiny parasols. I guess that was what I expected and it isn't that way at all. I have half a mind to collect my bags and try someplace else. If traffic weren't so hazardous I'd rent a car and go exploring on my own, perhaps all the way down to Miami."

She put her hand sympathetically on his arm, her face bending toward him. "I would hate to have you disappointed on your first trip to Florida, Mr. Hathaway." Her eyes brightened with a sudden inspiration. "Why don't you come with us? Donnie and

I are driving to Miami this afternoon. There's plenty of room. We'd be delighted to have you, wouldn't we, Donnie?"

"Huh! What?" Trask was bewildered. "What the hell?" He stopped, catching the slight compression of her lips. "Well, sure. Whatever you say." This Hathaway made him uneasy. Who the hell ever heard of riding with a cop unless you had to.

"My, Miss Lewis, but you are a delightful person; so fresh, so natural, so considerate. It would be pleasant to ride with you, really a rare opportunity."

"Well, then, it's settled. Where are your bags?"

"Just across the street, in the bus station. I'll get them. Only be a minute." He hurried out.

"Are you nuts?" Donnie wheeled upon her. "A cop!"

"That's right." Her eyes were following Mr. Hathaway. "A cop who's looking for Valenti. So we let him look and do the spade work. Where he is, we are. Simple? Let's get your car. By the way, my name is Lewis. Marcia Lewis." She laughed. "Mr. Hathaway thinks it is a pretty name."

CHAPTER FIVE

J*eff drove slowly* and with conscious relue-tance along the crushed-shell road skirting the heavy marsh. In this early morning a pearly mist hovered in undulating scarves over the greentipped reeds. Save for the sound of his car and the angry snarling of an outboard motor in the channel nothing intruded here. A lone pelican, roosting with sleepy patience atop a marker at the edge of a mud flat, was his only companion.

As he steadied the wheel against the pitted track he tried to resolve the problem with which he had been tormented for the past twenty-four hours. For the first time he disliked his job and was approaching a story with distaste. A stormy telephone conversation with Grant Burrows hadn't helped. Grant was impatient and, Jeff had to admit, not without provocation.

"How long are you going to sit on this, Martin?" That had been the tipoff. Jeff could never recall Burrows addressing him by his last name. "If you've got Cartright, I don't have to tell you it's the biggest story of the year. Why the hell are you holding me up?" The bellow of the question had not been muted by the distance separating them. "I'll tell you something. If you found him by accident then some jerk reporter from a country weekly could stumble across the same thing. Where will we be then?"

Jeff made a halfhearted attempt to parry the question. "I saw Valenti in West Palm Beach."

"To hell with Valenti!" It was a roar. "I want Judge Cartright and you've got him. Let's not write a mystery story about it. Just get me the facts; why he disappeared, what he has been doing all these years."

"Will you give me a little more time, Grant?" Jeff pleaded. "This all wraps up together—Valenti and Cartright."

"How do you know? Give me one good, sensible reason and no more of the crystal-ball stuff. You know I usually let you have your head but now you've got me chewing these anti-tension pills as if they were Life Savers. If someone else breaks this Cartright story I swear to God I'll cut your throat. I don't mean that figuratively either."

Jeff knew the man was right. He had no business to play it cozy simply because he had a hunch.

"Let me do it my way, will you, Grant?" Desperately he attempted to stave off the ultimatum he knew was on the tip of the city editor's tongue.

"How much is a little time, Jeff?" Burrows was weakening.

"I don't know." He didn't want to commit himself to a date. "I saw your friend Longworth in West Palm Beach. Valenti was on a chartered cruiser. We went out together but Valenti wouldn't talk. He doesn't like reporters."

"That's too damn bad. I hope he didn't hurt your feelings. Now, listen to me." The voice was crisp. "I'm going to let you have your way on this for a while longer. I'm a patient man, but there is a limit. If and when I decide you're stalling I'll send another boy down and you can come back and write obits. That's a promise." There was a brief silence and then Burrows's voice came across the wire again, softer this time. "Jeff?"

"Yep?"

"Don't think I'm acting like a city editor out of a movie." It was close to an apology. "You know what you've got as well as I do. If you were sitting in this chair and I was down there you'd be bouncing around a little too."

"I suppose so," he admitted unhappily. "I won't fumble it, Grant."

"All right." The acquiescence was granted wearily and the connection broken.

On his way to the Senator's houseboat now, Jeff tried to decide how to handle the story. Certainly it had to be done without emotion, impersonally. What was a boozy old man to him? He wished he had never come to Redemption Cay. Judge Cartright was a fumbling old rummy steeped these many years in some bitter tea of his own brewing. Here, in this remote spot, he had found a small measure of sanctuary from the things that haunted him. He was as much at peace as he would ever be. And Judy? Judy Carter who wasn't Judy Carter at all or even Judy Cartright. What is it going to do to her?

These were questions which he should not be asking himself. They were outside a column of newsprint. For a one-or-two-day sensation he and Grant Burrows were going to rip aside the veil of anonymity so carefully woven here. That was the function of a reporter and his obligation to the paper for which he worked. Just the same he felt lousy because he couldn't be honest with himself. Every instinct, everything he had learned about his craft warned him not to permit sentiment or a personal consideration to enter this. A pretty girl and an old man. Hell! The world was filled with them. That was what he told himself, but a tiny voice whispered persistently and would not be denied.

He parked the car in the small clearing within the high ground rising from the marsh and walked toward the creek where the houseboat was moored. The judge was sitting alone astride a small bench on the after deck. He looked up as the gangplank creaked beneath Jeff's weight. For a second he shaded his eyes, peering at the visitor. Then a quick smile of welcome broke over his face.

"Come aboard, my boy! Come aboard, and welcome!" He shouted although there was no need to raise his voice. He had been mending a cast net with which Judy caught shrimp in the shallow waters of the lagoon. It dropped in an untidy heap about his feet as he stood up. "Your visit is a welcome diversion from a housewives' task. The mending of nets belongs to St. Peter and to old crones."

"How are you?" Jeff took the outstretched hand.

"The answer can only be relative, my boy. To know how I am I must remember how I was. That is difficult. Sit down. Sit down." He pushed a camp stool toward Jeff. "I must thank you for the succor you rendered me the other night. A good Samaritan, indeed."

He waited until Jeff was seated, darted a quick, foxy glance over the marsh and the connecting waterways, then padded to the boat's stern. On his knees he bent over, reached down and took in a length of string between his fingers. Tied to the end, dripping with the creek's water, was a pint of whiskey. He held it to the light for inspection.

"It is surprising, sir, what these waters will yield. A rare catch indeed. You will join me, I hope."

"It's a little early, Senator."

"Nonsense, Mr. Martin. It is never too early or too late. Man must not permit himself to become a creature of habit. He should stand out boldly against the routine. It is his only hope of salvation." He hurried to the cabin and returned with a couple of glasses and a jug of water.

Jeff lit a cigarette, watching the play of huge dragonflies over the marsh. This was it. He couldn't avoid it. Maybe a drink would make it easier.

The Senator was craftily animated. "I am quite certain Judy knows of the existence of my remarkable fishing line at the stern, but she has achieved a wisdom beyond her years. Wisdom, understanding and tolerance—those things are not easily come by, my boy. She pretends it isn't there and I pretend she doesn't know."

"Judge Cartright." Jeff spoke the name distinctly.

The hands, busy with the stopper, halted their movement. The head remained bent over the task as it had been. Then, painfully, with an agonizing slowness, the fingers tightened and began to work out the cork. It came soundlessly, and the judge lifted his face. The eyes were bleak, the face stricken. Without a word he passed the bottle to Jeff, who poured a small drink. The judge then sat with the bottle clasped in both hands, staring at it, not seeing it.

"Who are you, Mr. Martin?" The words were dull, lifeless.

"I'm a reporter, Judge. The New York *Globe*." He shook his head. "And this is accidental. I didn't come looking for you. It was just one of those things a lucky newspaperman sometimes stumbles across."

Deliberately, trickling the liquor into his glass, Judge Cartright poured a drink. "After all this time, these many years." He spoke to himself unbelievingly. He swallowed the drink quickly. "It would be useless for me to deny it, I suppose. So, I can only ask what you propose to do."

"You know what I have to do, Judge. You know what you'd do if the roles were reversed."

The massive head rolled slowly. "No. I don't know what you have to do. I know what you will probably do."

"Will you tell me about it, Judge?"

There was dignity in the old man now. "Why should I assist you in ruining what is left of my life, Mr. Martin? Should I conspire with you to make miserable the little time remaining to me and a great deal of time left to Judy?"

"Who is Judy?"

"Judy is my daughter, Mr. Martin." The stare was flinty and the judge straightened in his chair, drawing upon a long unused source of strength.

"Uh-uh." Jeff brushed the answer aside. "You never had a daughter."

"My wife had a daughter, Mr. Martin."

Jeff was startled. He stared incredulously at the man.

"Who was her father?" He threw the question as he would a punch, hoping to rock the old man off balance.

The judge smiled wanly. "It won't do, Mr. Martin. I was a practicing attorney once and employed similar tactics with uncooperative witnesses. It won't do."

"Why did you disappear, Judge? Are you going to tell me what happened?"

"I am going to tell you nothing, Mr. Martin. I am no fugitive and need answer for my actions to no one but myself. Print what you like. I can't stop you. Crowd this peaceful spot with reporters and photographers. Sound the horn and bring the pack down in full cry. I will say to them what I say to you. This is not your affair."

"Edward Valenti was in West Palm Beach yesterday." Jeff was relentless. "I think he is looking for you, Judge Cartright."

"Why should you think that, Mr. Martin?"

"You sent Valenti to prison."

The smile was barely discernible, but it was there. "I sent a great many men to prison, Mr. Martin. None that I can recall ever cared to look me up after he was released."

"I'll tell you what I think, Judge." This was the shock approach and dangerous. Even a rummy could be tormented beyond his capacity to endure. "I think you double-crossed Valenti. I think you were reached before the trial ended. You were paid off.

"Why you took the money and jeopardized a brilliant career I have no way of knowing. But I think you took it and Valenti stood before you expecting a minimum sentence at the most or, if the money was big enough, a suspended sentence. But he didn't get it. You gave him the book. I think that is why you walked from your chambers and disappeared. I think that is why you soak yourself in whiskey, so you won't have to remember."

"If you are attempting to goad me into making a statement, Mr. Martin, you are wasting your time. Even if we should assume that your hypothesis is correct, it would still be a matter between Edward Valenti and me."

Jeff shook his head. He had to admire the old man's inflexibility. "You can't keep it between Valenti and you. There's Judy; what happens to her if Valenti gets to you?" He stood up, gazing almost compassionately down at the man.

"If you are suggesting that Mr. Valenti is here for the purpose of disposing of me, Mr. Martin, you are mistaken. It is probably the last thing he would want to do at the moment."

"What does that mean?" Jeff was puzzled.

"No more or less than what I said."

The even throb of a motor caused Jeff to turn his head. In the distance he could see Judy as she edged her boat into the canal's mouth.

"You'd better get rid of that whiskey."

The judge nodded, retied the neck to the string and dropped it over the side. He gathered up the glasses and water, dodging quickly into the cabin. Jeff waited as the boat approached, and lifted his hand in reply to the girl's waved greeting. Then she was alongside and a length of manila line spun out and fell at his feet.

"Hook me on, will you, sailor?" Her grin was impudent.

He experienced a warm glow of pleasure at the sight of her. "You mean, make it fast?"

"I didn't want to confuse you." She came lightly over the houseboat's rail and stood before him, her face uplifted. "Where have you been?"

"Oh, making like a tourist, riding around the country."

"I'm glad you're back." She made the statement unaffectedly and then looked around the deck. "Where's Pop? Didn't I see him out here?"

"He went below."

She stuck the tip of her tongue out at him. "You're learning. I expected you to say downstairs." Her eyes were bright. "If you're any good at cleaning fish, you can stay for breakfast. They were seining off the point by the inlet and I talked Joe Rattner out of half a dozen little pompano."

"I don't know." He was dubious as to his status aboard this boat now. "I'd like to. Maybe you'd better ask the judge."

She regarded him with a puzzled little frown. "The judge?"

"I mean the Senator." The slip was almost too hastily withdrawn. In an attempt to divert her he added, "I've never tried to clean a fish."

"You really don't know much, do you?" She left him with that and went over the railing again, clambering back with the fish wrapped in a piece of sacking. "Here. Catch." She tossed the bundle into his hands. "I sure don't know how anyone can grow up and not be able to clean a fish."

He drawled, "I know one thing and that is that you look like a lot more girl this morning than you did in those dungarees the other day." He regarded her with frank admiration, his eyes traveling over the clean, brown litheness of her legs and the unmistakable swell of firm breasts beneath the nylon blouse.

"Oh! These? I hoped someone would notice." She colored faintly, a gypsy flush beneath the even tan of her cheeks, and touched the edge of the very brief shorts, running the hem between her fingers. "They shrank some, I guess," she said with a grin.

Judge Cartright came from the cabin. His step was heavy, a weary man with a load of trouble. His expression lightened at the sight of Judy.

"Hello, girl."

She went to him quickly, raising herself on tiptoes to touch his cheek lightly with her lips. "Hi!" I went out early. You were still asleep. I have some fresh pompano. How about fish and grits for breakfast? I asked Mr. Martin to stay."

Jeff glanced at the judge, an unspoken question in his eyes. He was the intruder now, threatening the peace of those two. He waited unhappily for the judge's answer.

"Well, that's fine, girl. We don't have many guests. It's lonely for you. I'll just finish what I was doing here." He went over to his bench, picked up the cast net he had been mending and with needle in hand bent his head intently, peering at the rips.

Judy, puzzled, looked slowly from the judge to Jeff. "What's happened? Is something wrong?"

He wanted to tell her, knowing if he didn't speak now he would be forced to compound one lie or evasion with another until a wall was built between them. He shook his head. "Nothing. We were just talking until you came."

Her eyes met his steadily. She wasn't satisfied with the reply. Finally, she took the bundle of fish from his hands and indicated a bucket fastened to a length of line.

"Dip up a pail of water and bring it to me in the galley." She managed a worried smile. "I'll show you how to clean fish." She dropped lightly down the steps into the cabin and disappeared.

Jeff stood uncertainly for a moment, looking after her, then he swung the pail over the side. He hauled it up when it was full.

"Mr. Martin." The judge turned on his seat. Jeff waited. "It would be simple enough to order you off the boat, but it wouldn't solve anything, would it?"

"I'm afraid not, Judge." He made the admission reluctantly.

"No." The judge was thoughtful. "There is no solution. Certain things, beyond my control now, have been set in motion. To pretend to deny your existence solves nothing. Judy would be curious. She would ask questions and I would have to tell her. It is not a pleasant task you have put me to, Mr. Martin."

"You're going to have to tell her some time, anyhow, Judge."

"In my own time and in my own way. That is, if you will allow me the time. How much do I have? Hours? Days?"

"Not much, Judge." He was miserable. "My desk already knows what I know. They are not using it because I have held them off until I had the complete story."

"Your conscience doesn't bother you, Mr. Martin?"

"Does yours?" He was angry, defensive.

"It used to. Time has dulled it. I had almost forgotten who I was. It has been simpler to fade into the role of a town character, and like a good actor I have played my part both on and off the stage. Well." The heavy shoulders drooped and then straightened. "Let us be pleasant with one another. There is no point in useless recriminations. I do not dislike you, Mr. Martin, despite what you are about to do." He went back to his mending.

Jeff took the water into the cabin. At a sink in the corner galley Judy had the yellow and silver pompano split and cleaned. She washed them in the pail of water and then rolled them in corn meal. The coffee was on, grits bubbling softly. He stood beside her, his shoulder brushing her arm as she moved. He thought she was unaware of the contact and the sudden magic in it until she looked up and smiled with a fleeting shyness.

"I missed you. I think that's very strange, don't you?"

"It should be, but, somehow, it isn't."

"It's nice having you here." Her eyes sparkled. "I thought if I waited long enough someone would come by to hang on my garden gate. Now it's you and I don't know anything about you and it doesn't seem to make any difference."

"You don't know what you're saying." He was troubled by her seriousness.

"Yes, I do." She was infinitely wiser and older. "I suppose I should be fluttery and demure, except"— her smile was tender—"I'm not the downcast-eyes type. I'm not the dungaree and sweatshirt type either. I guess they were some sort of a defense against loneliness, a feeling of being incomplete."

"Even here there must have been boys, someone you liked."

"There have been boys, but I guess that sums it up. Living this way, just the two of us. Well, I guess you grow up in a hurry. What do you do, Jeff?"

"I'm a reporter. This was sort of a vacation. I live in New York."

"And when the vacation is over you'll go back to New York?"

"That's where I earn my living."

"Of course." She said it absently, lifting a lid from a pot and stirring the grits with a wooden spoon. Then she looked up and the shadow was gone from her face. "If you really meant what you said the other night, about taking me to the movies, I'd like to get dressed up in girl clothes. I really have them. Until now there hasn't been anyone to get dressed up for." She laughed. "And just in case you think I don't know any better, that sentence ended with a preposition."

"I split infinitives." He made the confession with mock seriousness.

She shook her head commiseratingly. "You'll never get any-place that way. Rail splitting, yes. Infinitive splitting, uh-uh."

The pompano had browned quickly in the deep fat, turning crisp. Judy forked them out to drain on a piece of paper and then prepared three plates, poured coffee and turned out the burners on the butane stove.

"Here." She handed him a plate and took the other two. "Let's eat outside."

They had breakfast on the deck in the warming sunshine while hungry sea birds swooped nervously and with shrill, eager cries, alert for the scraps which they tossed over the side. Now and then Jeff caught the girl's anxious, sidelong glances as she watched the judge. He was silent, preoccupied, eating without pleasure, his eyes fixed on some distant point. Finally she put her plate aside.

"Now." The demand was emphatic. "Tell me what's wrong. The two of you certainly don't know each other well enough to argue, so it must be something else."

"It isn't anything, Judy girl." The judge stood up. "I think I'll take a walk. Good-bye, Mr. Martin." He nodded briefly to Jeff.

They watched him without speaking as he crossed to the shore, moving along the worn path, a stark and lonely figure against the trembling expanse of marsh grass. He disappeared at a turn in the road.

"What happened here before I came? I know someone had a drink; I could smell it. But I don't care about that. There's something I don't know, something I should know." She waited.

"The judge will tell you."

"Why do you keep calling him the judge?" She was perplexed. "That's twice you said it this morning."

"Senator. Judge." He shrugged. "It's a natural error."

"I don't think it is a natural error at all." She was emphatic. "You either call him Senator, as everyone else in Redemption Cay does, or you call him Mr. Carter. You don't address him as Judge unless there's a reason. What's the reason, Jeff?"

"I told you it was a slip of the tongue." Unintentionally his voice was rough. He took a cigarette from his shirt pocket, lit it, handed it to her and then lit one for himself.

She sat, holding the cigarette between her knees. "I don't think I like you when you lie." She spoke calmly. "Besides, you do it so badly." Reluctantly, she stood up. "Let's wash the dishes. And don't think for a moment I have finished with my question. You'll tell me."

He washed, wiped and put away the few dishes while she tidied up the galley and then made the judge's bunk. Finished, she stood looking around, satisfied that everything was in order.

"If you don't have anything better to do, or even if you have, let's take my boat out and I'll try and make a sailor of you." She extended her hand and he took it.

"I don't want to be a sailor." He grinned, relieved that she no longer pressed him. "I want to be a farmer and walk through the fields of waving grain or whatever it is a farmer does."

She winked. "He has daughters so traveling salesmen can tell jokes about them. Didn't you know?"

The sun lay as a warm and filmy blanket over them. Judy, propped on one arm, traced a tickling path over his bare chest with a spray of sea oats. Their bodies were cradled in the clean, white sand of the beach and beyond, the ocean, with scarcely a murmur, washed pleasantly against the shore. Behind them, over a ridge of dunes, Judy's boat was moored within a secluded cove.

His hand closed over hers. "This doesn't seem much like a lesson in seamanship to me," he said.

"Oh! I don't know." She was airily unconcerned. "Sailors and girls. That is one of the first things you have to learn." A finger twisted and twined with one of his.

He smiled contentedly. "Out of the mouths of babes."

"I'm no babe. Not the kind you say 'Hello babe,' to. Or the kind you have to burp. Remember that and we'll get along just fine." She tossed the stalk of sea oats away, propped her elbows in the sand, resting her chin in cupped hands, staring down at him. "Have you ever been in love? I mean, how can you tell for sure? What does it feel like?"

"You're supposed to quiver like a plate of Jello."

"What flavor?" Her eyes widened.

"Strawberry." He was solemn.

"Well. That's it, then." Her sigh was one of relief. "It's strawberry all right."

He shook his head almost sadly. "You don't mean that, Judy. I don't want you to mean it."

"Why not?"

He smiled. "For one thing it isn't maidenly to talk that way."

"Well! You're certainly being as maidenly as someone's old aunt."

"That's it." He spoke quietly. "You're much too young, and I'm much too old."

"I'm not too young. I'm nineteen. What do you want, an old hag of twenty?" She was vehement. "Don't be so damn superior. How old are you?"

"Thirty. Thirty-one, if you want it in exact figures."

"An infant." She scoffed. "When I'm ninety you'll only be one hundred and two." She lowered her face and her cheek touched the corner of his mouth. She smelled, he thought, of sun, salt air and the fresh east wind. "Don't make fun of me, Jeff," she whispered. "What would I do with a boy of my own age? Don't you understand that my life hasn't been like that of other girls?"

"With a boy of your age or near it you could go to the movies, hold hands, eat popcorn, listen to rock 'n' roll records."

"I can hardly wait. What's the matter, don't you like popcorn?" She slid from her elbows with a flowing, liquid movement until her head rested within the hollow of his arm, her face against his.

"Do you know what you're doing?" He felt her soft, moist breath on his mouth.

"I'm courting you." He could feel her silent laughter. "It's brazen but nice and I don't think it'll do you any good to scream. I know what I'm doing. A woman always knows."

"Oh! So you're a woman now?"

"If that's a nice-nelly way of trying to find out if I'm a virgin the answer is yes. Not that I attach any particular virtue to the condition. It's just that I never cared enough about anyone before."

"You don't know what you are saying." Even as he protested his arm tightened about her.

She moved almost sleepily against him and he could feel the ripple of a spasmodic tremor as it raced through her body.

A sea gull wheeled with alert curiosity above them, peered down with its bright, beady eyes and then swooped away with a keening sound of excitement.

CHAPTER SIX

*O**n the main*** street of Fort Lauderdale, Donnie came out of a drugstore, the cigarettes he had purchased unopened in his hand. He settled hastily behind the wheel and his foot tapped warningly on Marcia's ankle.

"The goon. Booker. In the drug store." He whispered the words as he bent his head to turn on the ignition. "Where Booker is, the boat and Valenti are."

Her hand tightened cautioningly on his arm. For a moment she stared straight ahead, thinking, planning. Finally, she turned and spoke to Mr. Hathaway in the back seat.

"I'm terribly sorry." She was sincerely apologetic. "Would it inconvenience you, Mr. Hathaway, if we decided not to go on to Miami after all? Donnie—Donnie telephoned some friends while he was in the drugstore and they insist we stay with them for a few days."

"My goodness, no, Miss Lewis. To have had your delightful company this far has been a privilege. I have enjoyed the ride tremendously. I wouldn't want you to put yourself out for a stranger. Now! I'll just take my bags." He moved with alacrity to the sidewalk. I'll take my bags and have a taxi run me over to the bus station."

"I'm sorry." She gestured regretfully. "But it isn't far from here to Miami and the bus ride is comfortable."

"Don't apologize at all. This was an unexpected pleasure. It is not often that I am permitted the company of two such delightful young persons." He tipped his hat formally and then hurried along the sidewalk, the suitcases banging awkwardly against his legs.

Marcia's attention was on the drugstore's entrance and she felt Donnie's elbow nudge her as the tall, shuffling figure of Booker emerged. He stood blinking in the sunlight, his head swinging to follow the progress of each girl as she passed. He unwrapped a package of gum and stuffed all five sticks into his mouth. Then, he lumbered along, his jaws working stolidly on the wad.

Donnie backed out slowly, merging with the stream of traffic while Marcia half rose in the seat to keep Booker in sight.

In the rear of a cab Mr. Hathaway leaned forward. His eyes were bright with anticipation.

"Now." He instructed. "That convertible just pulling out. Please follow it; discreetly, of course, but keep it in sight." At the skeptical expression on the man's face he made a reassuring sound. "It's quite all right. There is nothing sinister in what we are doing. They are friends of mine."

The driver shrugged indifferently and wheeled to join the slowly moving cars. It wasn't any of his business. A fare was a fare. But, if like the little fellow said, they were friends why didn't he ride with them? There was the whole back seat empty.

Booker moved with an elephantine heaviness, crossing a bridge over the New River and then to a cement walk bordering the waterways. Boats, large and small, were moored here almost bow to stern. He regarded their occupants with a faint sneer. Boats were for jerks and the ones who owned them were always polishing, varnishing or washing down the decks with a hose and mops. Besides, there wasn't any room and you had to keep looking at the same faces every day.

Booker's mind worked as ponderously as his body. He felt a gnawing resentment over his status. The old man was at him all the time like he was a servant. He figured to be a bodyguard, maybe with a gun. But the old man never left the damn boat, so what did he need a bodyguard for? Besides, whenever there was anything to do it was Spain who took over. He distrusted smart joes like Valenti, Spain and stuff like that Doris. They always had a crack ready, and by the time he thought of an answer they were talking about something else. Doris was the worst, jabbing at him all the time, talking in front of the others like he wasn't there.

A slow, smouldering rage was building itself within him. He spent his days mentally raping Doris. It was a brutal rape in which he beat her until she screamed and fell to her knees, clinging to his legs and pleading. She would crawl. He licked his lips. She wouldn't be so wise then. She'd crawl, begging him to do it to her. But he wouldn't, not right away. He'd make her ask and ask. When he was good and ready he'd rip her clothes off and in the end just leave her lying there, naked and calling for him to come back. Sometimes Booker thought he'd like to dig his thumbs into her neck until her eyes popped like grapes. Then he wanted to dirty and humiliate her. It made him feel good just to think about it.

On the cruiser Valenti was comfortably stretched out in a deck chair. Doris was perched on a railing, posing for the men working on nearby boats, her long legs swinging with a calculated indolence. As he crossed the gangway Booker thought she looked nakeder in those shorts than most women did without any clothes on at all. He had a special, four letter word for Doris and he said it to himself now with moist satisfaction.

"Hi, ape." Doris leaned back against a stanchion, regarding him with a mocking expression of dreamy sensuality. "Did you get your comic books and bubble gum?"

"Ahhh!" He growled. "Nuts to you."

"Boy!" She was breathless with admiration. "Are you sharp with the uptake." She addressed Valenti, who regarded her with a frown. "No matter what you say about Booker," she continued, "he's always in there punchy!"

"Stop riding Hal, Doris. I've spoken to you about it before. Leave him alone." He wondered if she understood how dangerous this plodding hulk could be. His was the slow wrath of a brute and it would be senseless and crushing.

"Hell." Doris was unconcerned. "I thought you brought him along for the laughs. Give me a cigarette, ape."

"You know I don't smoke. I gotta keep in shape. You know that." He flexed his hands and muscles proudly.

The staccato tapping of high heels on the slip caused Doris to glance up. There was a small light of surprise in her eyes at the sight of the girl who turned on to the gangway and, without asking permission or displaying hesitation, came aboard. Valenti partially raised himself from his chair and turned his body.

"Mr. Valenti?" She stood before him.

Valenti noted every detail of the trim, tailored figure. Finally he nodded.

"I'm Jim Harper's sister."

"So?"

Marcia glanced from Booker to Doris. "I'd like to talk with you—alone."

Doris sniffed but made no move to leave her perch on the rail.

"You want I should put her off, boss?" Booker swayed his heavy body with pleased anticipation.

"How do I know you are Harper's sister or why should it interest me?"

"You know I'm Harper's sister because I say so." Her brief smile was untroubled.

Valenti continued to study her. Then he nodded. "Doris, you and Hal take a walk."

Doris hesitated and then swung from the railing with an easy grace. "Sure. Come on, ape. I'll let you climb some coconut trees." She crossed the gangway with a ripple of hips and, after a moment, Booker shuffled slowly after her.

"What do you want?" Valenti didn't invite her to sit down but she took a chair and lit a cigarette slowly.

"What do you think I want?" She allowed the smoke to drift lazily from half-parted lips.

"Michael," Valenti called in the direction of the cabin and when the man appeared Valenti indicated the girl. "Do you know her?"

Spain nodded without hesitation. "She was Harry Blake's wife. Jim Harper's sister."

"Thank you, Michael." Spain returned to the cabin. "Just answer my question. I asked what you wanted?"

"Jim's share." She leaned back, crossing her legs, waiting.

"Your brother talked too much." The voice grated. "Some of the talk sent me to prison. I didn't like that. It was unnecessary. He has nothing coming."

"I say he has."

"You're wasting your time, Mrs. Blake. There is nothing to cut up."

"For the time being the name is Marcia Lewis, and there will be something to cut up when you find what you came down here for."

"Are you threatening me?" He was curious, eyeing her again with more attention.

"The great Valenti?" She snapped the half-smoked cigarette over the rail. "Well, maybe I am. Jim is in prison because of that money. He—we—only want what is coming. There is plenty for everyone if you're not greedy. Don't think you can scare me off with Mike Spain or this fellow Booker. If I have to I can hire man for man to match them."

"You're a fool." Involuntarily he raised his voice. "No one talks to me that way."

"I do." She was unimpressed. "By the way—and I'm telling you this only because we have a common interest— there is a cop following you, a little man whose name is Hathaway. This is a hunch. He came down on the train with me." Rapidly she sketched Mr. Hathaway's movements from the time he arrived in Palm Beach. "I'm not sure why I tie him in with this but I do."

"Does he know who you are?"

"No. At least, I don't see how he could. I never saw him before."

Valenti was a superstitious man. For reasons which he couldn't explain this girl made him uneasy. Some people carried trouble the way others walked around with typhoid fever, passing it on. She was trouble. He could smell it. Too many persons were edging into the picture.

In the beginning only he and Michael had known why this trip to Florida was made. Now, he mentally counted them off. There was this girl, and a cop, if she was right. A reporter from a New York paper sniffing around and, maybe, even that deputy sheriff in West Palm Beach. He couldn't take anything for granted and he wondered where it had started to go wrong. Even this boat was no longer a good idea. In the beginning he had liked the plan. It was a retreat, a base. Now it had become a liability. He sighed without sound. He must get rid of the boat and, probably, the girl also. He was becoming impatient and knew this was dangerous. None of the sources of information from which he had hoped to draw had been worth a damn. There was nothing but rumor. He was chasing a ghost, a ghost loaded with a million and some dollars. No one suspected how much he needed that money. He couldn't afford to let anyone know. That was when you could get kicked in the guts.

"Well?" She interrupted his thoughts impatiently.

"I don't need you." He spoke roughly, but there was no conviction behind the words. "I have to avoid complications. You are an unexpected one." He was irritated by his indecision. That was what prison had done. You got regimented, doing the same thing every day at the same time. After a while you even stopped thinking for yourself. He felt an almost irresistible desire to scream his frustration, the way guys did when they went stir crazy.

"I don't want to complicate it." Her words were even. "All I want is Jim's share. We don't have to have trouble unless you want it that way."

"Michael," Valenti called again and Spain came quickly as though he had expected the summons. "Sit down, Michael." The command was given almost wearily. "We have a guest." He indicated the girl.

Marcia's eyes narrowed suspiciously and she waited for Spain's reaction. The man was studying the title page of a book with detached interest.

"The boat won't do, Michael." Valenti's tone seemed to gather authority. "It was my idea, but a bad one. We are too conspicuous. Miss Lewis wasn't my idea but she is here. Get the captain, Michael."

Spain laid aside his book, went forward and returned with McElroy.

"Sit down, Captain." Valenti was almost gracious. "We have decided to give up the cruise. There is no question of returning any of the money. The arrangements which Mr. Spain made with you still stand. But I realize I will be more comfortable ashore."

"I didn't think you were having much fun or getting what you paid for." Secretly, McElroy was relieved. The setup was getting on his nerves. There was something wrong, something he couldn't name. On the way down he had thought it over.

"Now." Valenti was once more commanding. "I want you to think, Captain. I would like a place somewhere along the coast where a cottage or house could be rented. I want privacy, so I don't want a resort. It needs to be small, an island would be fine, but something near enough to the mainland so we could reach it by a small boat. Have you a suggestion?"

In McElroy's mind a chart of the coast from St. Lucie's Inlet to Key Largo was spread out. Some places he rejected immediately. "You don't want to stay in a town? There are some small places. You'd be more comfortable."

"I want nothing but privacy. I have been uncomfortable before."

"I know a place. It's north from here. Across the river is the beach, a long narrow island really. There are cottages there and one or two larger houses. It's close enough to the mainland so you can go in or have supplies brought over but it's pretty wild and lonely. You'd sure as hell be private there."

"These cottages, are they occupied?"

"No-o-o. I wouldn't guess so at this time of year. Mostly they rent during the summer months to folks who come to the ocean from the interior or Georgia. Winter tourists are more like for hotels and those motels and trailer camps. I'd almost figure you'd be the only people on the beach now. We could get hold of a real estate man who'd tell you what's available."

"Thank you, Captain." Valenti waited until McElroy had left. "What do you think, Michael?"

Spain was silent, thoughtful. Then he nodded. "It's better." He regarded Marcia steadily. "What about her?"

"We are having enough trouble without adding to it, Michael. We let Miss Lewis in. It doesn't please me, but—" He shrugged.

"Don't do me a favor." She was angry. "Jim's entitled to his share. He wants me to have it."

"Harper talked himself out of any share he had coming. I'm making a deal now because it seems smart. You can come with us or get off the boat. I don't care. I'm not going to argue."

She studied him and then nodded. "I'll come with you. I have a friend."

Valenti shook his head. "No friend. It's you alone or not at all. You're in no position to bargain."

"The hell I'm not." She tried to make it sound determined.

Valenti glanced at his watch. "I'll give you exactly one minute to make up your mind."

Her mind raced ahead. This was what she had come to Florida for, to find Valenti and stay with him. He was making it easy; maybe too easy, she couldn't be sure about that. It had been a gamble all the way. She could either give up her seat and go home or draw cards.

"I'll stay." A wry grin forced itself reluctantly. "But I'd just as soon go swimming in a tank with sharks. I have some bags in the car. Just to keep it clean and friendly, my friend will know that I left here with you on this boat. He'll begin to ask questions if I don't turn up in a reasonable length of time."

Valenti's stare was hooded. "We'll get along better if you stop trying to threaten me. I'm not used to it."

She stood before him, slim and calmly defiant. Their eyes met and held. Finally she nodded and without a word turned and recrossed the gangway.

Spain slowly lifted his gaze to follow her and his lips pursed. "Trouble."

"Trouble either way, Michael." Valenti appeared almost happy. "But if we keep it with us we can keep it controlled. I can always count on you. Tell the captain to leave when he's ready." He paused, chewing at his lip speculatively. "And Michael, keep an eye on Hal. He is snorting like a bull." The thin lips twisted in a half smile. "And I have always said that Doris was a beautiful cow."

On a bench in a small palm-shaded park overlooking the river, Mr. Hathaway sat, giving a brightly critical attention to a game of checkers being played at an adjoining table. His eyes, however roved frequently to the *Oriole II*. The cab had been dismissed with a large tip and instructions to have the bags checked at the bus station and the stubs left in an envelope to be called for.

He had watched with pleased interest as Marcia Lewis went aboard the cruiser. Now his gaze followed her as she walked with brisk determination to where the convertible was parked. She stood, for a moment, talking to the man behind the wheel and once she even stamped her foot. This amused Mr. Hathaway. It was one of the completely feminine gestures which a modern world had not altered. They were arguing and she finally jerked the door open, pulled the suitcases from the back and started back along the walk toward the cruiser. The man in the convertible roared it about in a tight circle and disappeared.

Mr. Hathaway rose from the bench and hurried a little so his and the path of Miss Lewis should intercept. His smile was one of bright and delighted innocence.

"Miss Lewis. We meet again. Allow me to help you with those bags." He reached tentatively.

The suitcase swung in a short arc and banged viciously against Mr. Hathaway's shin.

"Get the hell away from me you—you creep!" The anger and contempt slashed at him.

With a sadly reproving cluck Mr. Hathaway watched as she strode away. Miss Lewis, he told himself, despite her associations and antecedents, was far too pretty and intelligent a girl to indulge in such common expressions. Then, he wondered if he really did appear as a creep. The word had a most unpleasant sound. He went back to his bench in a depressed mood and was indifferent to the annoyed glances of the checker players who were disturbed by his intrusion.

Miss Marcia Lewis and Mr. Edward Valenti. He chuckled inwardly. My, what an item that would make for the society columns. The fancy amused him and he began to compose a paragraph.

"Friends in San Quentin, Dannemora, Folsom, Sing Sing and Atlanta will be interested to learn of the cruise in southern waters being taken by Mr. Edward Valenti and the charming and delightful widowed sister of Mr. James Harper, Esq., a well known resident of Alcatraz."

He laughed aloud and one of the checker players hissed balefully. Mr. Hathaway smiled benignly at the man. He was in an excellent humor again. It was his private opinion that Miss Lewis was being most imprudent. But the stakes were considerable and it was quite possible that before this was all over he, also, would be forced to certain dangerous but well-considered acts. The knowledge did not particularly disturb him. However, he would give a lot to know where that cruiser was going.

Mr. Hathaway stood up. From long experience he had learned one simple, elementary fact. If you went around asking enough questions you sooner or later came up with some surprising answers.

Before leaving the bench he succumbed to an impulse. He leaned over the table and with a forefinger pushed a checker from one square to the next, setting up a double jump. Then, smiling brightly, he nodded and strolled away, indifferent to the outraged cry of the players. The memory of this sustained him for several trying hours.

The wake of the *Oriole II* fanned out in a lacy, foaming train. Marcia Lewis stood watching it, feeling a similar turmoil. Her eyes shifted now and then to the purpling shore, but they were without interest.

"Hi!"

She turned quickly, startled by the voice. Doris was regarding her with a speculative attitude. There had been no attempt made at introductions when she came aboard. She had gone forward to sit on a hatch in contemplative silence and remained there until she was chilled, lonely and even a little frightened. McElroy had glanced at her with curiosity a couple of times and once she had smiled faintly. When she went to the afterdeck it was deserted and she remained there, trying to see far enough ahead to plan.

Doris dropped lazily into a chair, her eyes slanted upward in Marcia's direction. "Don't get the idea, doll, that I'm a woman's woman looking for talk. I just said hi because I couldn't think of anything else to say. To hell with you."

Marcia's expression lost some of its tautness. She made a gesture of apology with one hand.

"Sorry." A brief smile went with it. "Hi yourself."

Doris yawned, stretched and scratched idly in the vicinity of her navel. She was satisfied with the reply and her curiosity was piqued.

"Are you just on for a local stop or making the grand tour?"

"I'm making the tour, I guess." Marcia seated herself.

"Boy!" Doris's expression brightened. "Are you in for some surprises. Who gets you, the ape or the spook Michael?" She leaned forward and continued with mocking humor. "I'm the star passenger. I get Valenti. He carries me around the way you would a diaphragm just in case you want to use it."

Marcia laughed honestly and without constraint. She relaxed and fished within her purse for a cigarette, regarding Doris with awakening interest.

"I'm Marcia." She offered Doris a cigarette and lit one for herself. "Marcia Lewis."

"That's all right." Doris leaned back. "We don't go in much for names. Most of the time you don't get spoken to at all."

"That suits me." Marcia lifted her face to the afternoon's waning sun. "That suits me fine."

Doris was silent for a moment. "You look pretty silly in that suit." She spoke abruptly. "I mean a suit aboard this scow. Jesus!" She breathed her admiration. "I'm sure getting nautical."

"I have some other stuff in the bags." Marcia was indifferent. "I didn't feel like changing."

A shadow fell across the deck and Doris twisted to look over her shoulder. Her eyes lighted with an almost diabolical joy and she straightened up quickly.

"Good evening, *Mr.* Ape." She greeted him with a burlesque falsetto of girlish innocence and smiled at him with demure sweetness.

"Huh?" Booker regarded her stupidly.

"Can't you see we got company." Her tone sharpened. "That's why I call you *Mr.* Ape. Don't you have any God-damned manners?" Her pose changed to the fancied dowager. "Join us, won't you?" She lifted her hand with regal condescension and turned to Marcia. "Marcia, may I present Mr. Hal Booker, the well known sportsman? Mr. Booker, Miss Marcia of the House Of All Nations."

"Hi yuh?" Booker was slightly dazed but he thrust out an enormous hand.

"Charmed, I'm sure." With an effort Marcia kept her face grave and extended her fingertips daintily. "Hi yuh?"

"I heard about the House Of All Nations." Booker wanted to put her at ease. "It's in Cuban someplace."

"How delightful that you know, Mr. Booker." Marcia's eyes were wide with surprise. "You must visit us some time. The mater will be enjoyed."

"Who's the mater?" Booker was floundering.

"That's Cuba for my mother." Her eyes were solemn pools.

"Aw! You're kiddin'." Booker was embarrassed. "Not your old lady too?"

Marcia nodded. "My father also." She was wistful with the memory. "He takes those pictures for postcards."

"Well, what do you know about that?" Booker was impressed. "How about it? You an' the old lady hustlin' an' the old man takin' pictures." Suddenly there was consternation on his face as he remembered something. "Hey! The old man wants you should come downstairs for a drink. I almost forgot."

"Did he say to tell them or those?" Marcia waited with alert attention.

Booker struggled with this. "Well, he said them, but"— he jerked a thumb in the direction of Doris—"he wants her, too, so I guess youse both better come."

Doris languidly extended her hand to Booker. "Assist me to arise, will you, Mr. Ape?"

With a blank expression Booker took her hand and Doris rose easily, smoothing modestly at her naked legs before bowing formally to Marcia.

"Will youse join us, Miss Marcia, in the saloon?"

"Charmed." Marcia also extended her hand to the surprised Booker.

"You see, you God-damned ape." Doris was gently reproving. "This is going to be an instructive cruise. You're going to get some God-damned culture if it kills you."

CHAPTER SEVEN

nbound through the choppy waters of the inlet the boat slewed and bucked, darting off on erratic tangents that threatened to put it hard on one of the many unpredictable sandbars. The wheel bucked beneath Jeff's unsure hands and he finally turned to Judy with a helpless grimace.

"You take her. I'll never learn. I'm more like for automobiles or scooters."

She shook her head, face lifted, eyes shining with pleasure. There was no mockery in her now, only happiness and a small, bright pride. He felt the slender warmth of her body as her cheek rested confidently for a second against his bare arm and she pressed against him.

"You're doing fine. Better than I did at first. Anyhow, I wouldn't care if we were wrecked. We could pretend the beach was a desert island. We'd scrounge around for food. Pretty soon our clothes would rot away and we wouldn't have to wear any. I'd like that fine."

His gaze softened on the tumbling waters ahead. "I don't know how a girl like you can think about such things."

Her whistle was derisive. "Girls think about such things all the time. The man they want, a chance to be alone with him."

Thrust by the flooding tide, the boat seemed to slide downhill through the last hundred feet or so of breakers and into the placid waters of the lagoon. In almost the same way, he thought, had their relationship been brought to this complete understanding; smoothly, effortlessly. He had been disturbed at first.

She had seemed so young, so eager for life, so vulnerable. Yet, he understood now that she was a woman with a woman's sure instinct and mature desires. Looking back to that first day on the beach he could find no cheap moment. She had given herself willingly, naturally, as though what was happening came from the deep and secret well of her life. She had looked upon him and herself unashamed; finding only wonder in what had happened.

Glancing at her now, moved as always by her dusky beauty and glowing vitality, he experienced the gnawing of his conscience. There were hours, such as those of today, when he could forget completely who and what he was. He was going to hurt her, strip her bare for the gloating of hot eyes. He was going to transform her and the judge into so many columns of type and drive them from this small Eden to stand within the pitiless glare of publicity. He was going to do this because he could no longer help himself. Burrows wouldn't wait while he lay in the sun making love to Judy, temporizing, inventing excuses. The ultimatum was always there, no farther away than the telephone on the city desk. Do the job for which you are being paid or move over and I'll send another man down. That was what Grant would say and, in his heart, Jeff could find no valid protest. He alone had started this and he would have to see it through.

"What are you thinking about?" She had become sensitive to his moods, looking at him now with a troubled doubt. "Sometimes you go away from me. I don't realize what's happening but suddenly you're not there."

His arm about her shoulders drew her to him. "I was thinking about you." The pressure lightened. He felt the need of making this protective gesture, knowing he had been betraying her in his mind. "I think about you most of the time."

"That's good." She smiled again. "I sound smug, don't I? Well, I am."

A crystal silence enveloped the river and the wonder of it never ceased to be a wonder, familiar now but, somehow, always new. The soft, copper radiance of a lowering sun, the bright green of the mangrove banks with now and then the startling whiteness of an egret in motionless alabaster atop the dark tangle. Beyond, the small town, a cardboard cut-out. Even the slow beat of the engine seemed to muffle itself, blending with the afternoon, and in the calm waters the wheel needed only a touch of a finger.

He moved a little to one side. "Take her in. I'll smoke a cigarette."

"From here she'll take herself in." She watched as his hands cupped the match's flame.

He leaned forward on his elbows. "Judy? How do you live? I mean what do you and the jud—the Senator do about money? The few fish you sell to Norn, the occasional tourist you take out fishing, those can't be enough."

Although he did not turn his head he could feel the question in her eyes, the rebellious stiffening of her body.

"That's a funny question to ask, and not funny funny either."

"Maybe so."

She thought this over for a moment, and then her tongue thrust against her cheek. Looking at her quickly he knew she was suppressing a giggle.

"I suppose," she conceded dryly, "you are entitled to know what my prospects are. After all, a man has to think of his future. Well, I'll tell you. I'm an eccentric heiress, just a madcap girl who gave it all up for this simple life."

Regretting the question, he was willing to let it go at that. She reached over and took the cigarette from his mouth, drew upon it and replaced it, her fingers touching his lips caressingly.

"I don't know." She mused. "I don't suppose I ever thought much about it. We've always had enough, never too much but never too little either. I know that the people in the Cay think we live in a shanty boat but it isn't. You've seen it. We live there because we like it. Money?" She spoke the word as though saying it for the first time. "Why, I don't know, Jeff, honestly. I guess Pop has some sort of annuity. Around the first of every month he gets a letter from a law firm in New York. It's the only mail we ever get and the only thing he has never talked with me about. He takes it to the bank himself so I suppose it contains a check. Then the bills we have run up at the stores are paid. He gives me the money for them. The extra cash we keep on the boat and I have to hide it sometimes when he's having one of his spells. But money as money never really occurred to me before."

"I'm sorry I asked. It's none of my business."

"No." She agreed solemnly. "It isn't, but I don't mind."

He was ashamed of himself. Never had she intruded upon his life or presumed beyond what he wanted to tell her. She had made no reservations. Never had she asked: What happens now? What happens when your vacation is up and you go back to New York. Do you have a girl there? Do you really love me or is this just what someone else would think it is? How is it to be a man and have a girl in love with him, knowing it is very possible that he will walk out of her life in a few weeks? Those were the things she might have asked and there were questions for which he had no answer.

"I salvaged this boat." Obliquely she was trying to answer his question. "It was adrift in the inlet. I had taken one of Mr. Norn's outboards and got a line on her and brought her in. She was waterlogged and a little beat up. We reported it to the Coast Guard but no one ever came to claim it. So Mr. McDonald helped me fix her up and then Mr. Norn got hold of a good second-hand motor cheap. They call her a Seabright dory, or that's what Mr. McDonald said. So," her tone became moody, "I guess I'm not really a madcap heiress after all."

The river narrowed here and as they rounded a tip of land just above the entrance to the Cay they both saw the boat at the same time. She lay at anchor, beautiful in the waning sun, her metal work and mahogany softly washed with its color, the hull spotlessly white. The tide swung the cruiser slowly about and the gold lettering on the stern was plainly visible: *Oriole II. W. Palm Beach, Fla.*

"She's beautiful." Judy was ecstatic. "I know her. That's Captain McElroy. He's been in here a couple of times before and I've seen her go through for years."

When he thought about it later Jeff realized he had felt no surprise. The cruiser had to be here; not this day, perhaps, but one morning, one afternoon, he would look out and see her. It was for this that he had argued and pleaded with Burrows; the following of a long hunch. Now, studying the lines of the boat, he knew that Edward Valenti was aboard and somewhere in Redemption Cay, at the bar of the Fish Shack or on the houseboat, was Judge Amos Cartright. Although the afternoon was warm he suddenly felt chilled.

Judy touched the wheel and the boat moved alongside the cruiser. A man forward on the deck shaded his eyes for a second and then lifted one hand.

"Hi Judy."

"Hi Captain McElroy." She cut the motor and dropped it into neutral. "What are you doing down here?"

"Charter, Judy. Is old man Norn around?"

"You can find him at the dock, I guess. Nice to see you again."

They moved ahead again and past the cruiser, Judy turning for a last look at her sleek magnificence.

"That's too good a boat for charter." She spoke to herself and then addressed him with a grin. "If I owned her I wouldn't let anyone aboard except you and Pop."

He was only half listening, obsessed with the sensation of some murky evil. The very absence of anyone except McElroy on the deck added to the illusion. It was as though within the gleaming hull dark threads were being woven into a net of cunning. He wanted to say to Judy, Get out of here; you and the judge leave this place. Don't ask why. Just go and go quickly.

"Should I drop you off at Norn's?" Judy asked. When he didn't reply she turned wonderingly. "Something wrong?"

He started and then forced a smile. "Nothing. What did you say?"

"I asked if you wanted me to drop you off at Norn's or will you come down and have supper with us?"

"No. You'd better leave me at the dock."

"Will you be down later?"

He hesitated. "I don't think so." At the look of surprise he made an attempt to amend the blunt statement. "I—I have to talk with New York tonight and I'm not sure when I'll be able to catch Burrows. He's my city editor. It may be late."

She nodded, swinging the craft in toward Norn's. "You are probably the clumsiest liar I ever listened to." She grinned. "I sort of like it because I'll always know when you're doing it."

She left him at the dock and he stood watching until the boat disappeared around an elbow of land. Then he walked slowly back to the hotel, entering the lobby and halting abruptly to stare at the figure slouched in one of the worn rattan chairs.

"What the hell are you doing here?"

The lanky figure of Jim Patrick, the *Globe*'s top photographer, unwound himself.

"Hi, Scoop." He grinned. "The old man sent me down." On the floor, beside the chair, was the inevitable case and camera. Patrick would as soon think of going out into the street without his trousers as to move without the equipment. "What have you got?"

Jeff was angry, knowing Burrows was deliberately crowding him. It wasn't Patrick's fault. This was an assignment, nothing more.

"I've got a drink in my room."

Upstairs, over bourbon in water tumblers, they talked shop for a few minutes and then Patrick lit a cigarette, leaning against the bureau and eyeing Jeff quizzically.

"You're stalling me, Jeff." He made the statement without any particular emphasis. "We've covered a lot of stuff together and this is the first time I ever knew you to hold out. What gives?"

At the window, Jeff was staring over the river. Save for the *Oriole II* it was empty, motionless, a leaden sheet in the gathering twilight.

"What did Grant tell you?" He spoke without turning.

"He said you'd fill me in. I thought he acted pretty cagey."

Jeff nodded wearily, moving from the window to pour himself another drink before replying. He knew he had to level with Patrick. More than that he had to level with himself.

"Do you remember the Judge Cartright disappearance?"

Patrick was suddenly alert. "Yeah." He spoke softly but there was a tenseness in his attitude.

"I found him. He's here, been living here for years. Calls himself Carter." He halted Patrick's exclamation with a shake of his head. "Let me finish. I'll give it all to you." Rapidly he covered the salient points for the photographer. He told him about the judge, Judy, Valenti's appearance in the river, and even about Deputy Sheriff Longworth in West Palm Beach. He tried to do it impersonally, coldly and factually. "That's it and now you know why Burrows didn't want to say anything, even to you." He shoved the bottle toward Patrick.

The man shook his head incredulously as he splashed some whiskey into his glass. "How do you like that?" He marveled. "There have been a hundred theories but they all spelled murder. He had a lot of strange connections." He squinted wisely at Jeff.

"The girl, Judy, she sort of got you, didn't she?"

Jeff's short laugh was without humor. "Does it show?"

"It shows." The photographer grinned.

"All right." He admitted. "The girl and, maybe, even the judge. I'm going to louse them up. It's the first time I ever stalled Grant. What would you do?"

"I'd do what you're going to do. Wrap it up and hand it to Burrows. So. Where's the judge? I'll take my little Brownie and we'll get some pictures."

"In the morning, Jim." It was close to a plea. He was fighting for time, knowing it was useless now. With or without him, Jim Patrick would find Judge Cartright in Redemption Cay. "Are you checked in here?"

"Yeah." Patrick wasn't satisfied. "Yeah. I'm checked in here." His eyes held Jeff's. "Don't try and kid me, Scoop. Don't make like a crime reporter on television." Some of the easy friendliness was gone. "Don't be cozy."

"In the morning, Jim." He was resigned. "In the morning I'll take you down to where they live. That's my word."

Patrick nodded. "That's good enough, Jeff." Once again he was his amiable self. "Where do you eat around here?"

Jeff stubbed out his cigarette. "The hotel is on the American plan but you can pass up the food without too much pain. There's a place down the street, a bar and grill. I usually go there in the evening."

"Well. I'm hungry. Let's shove off." He slung the camera case over his shoulder by its strap.

"You won't need that tonight." Jeff objected.

Patrick shook his head with a wise smile, slapping the case. "Where Daddy goes Baby goes."

In the lobby the hotel's owner, Abernathy, looked up from behind the desk. He was a rabbit of a man and at the moment his nose seemed to twitch with excitement.

"Business is certainly picking up." He chortled and rubbed his hands together. "Yes sir, it looks like a boom season for sure. Three guests at the same time. You an' your friend goin' to be here for supper, Mr. Martin?"

"No. I think we'll eat out. Patrick wants to see the town."

"Well, now, that's too bad. I just registered another guest. I thought maybe you'd all like to eat at the same table; sort of company for each other. Nice fellow, he seemed to be." Abernathy squinted at the ruled page of the old fashioned, ledger-type register. "Just come in late this afternoon. Man by the name of Hathaway."

In the main cabin of the cruiser, Doris was curled morosely in a chair, her angry eyes following Valenti as he paced restlessly up and down. Marcia, in a corner of the divan, was reading, indifferent to the company or her surroundings. As Michael entered Valenti halted abruptly.

"Well?" Valenti was impatient.

"McElroy's ready to take me ashore now," Michael answered.

"You know what's to be done." There was a rasping edge of irritation in Valenti's voice. "It's late but this is a small town and you can find a renting agent or real estate man at his home. Close it up, Michael, close it up. Find out about renting a small boat, too, and don't answer any questions. Just get the house and a boat. In the morning you can put in an order at the grocery store. I want to get off this damn boat. Do you understand?" Almost imperceptibly the tone rose to a hysterically shrill note.

Marcia glanced up with a faintly amused scorn. The spectacle of Valenti stripped of his icy calm filled her with a quiet contempt. She stared at him and went back to her reading.

"Do you want someone, a woman, to take care of the house?" Michael was undisturbed.

"I don't want anyone!" Valenti shouted. "Booker and Doris can do the work. Damn little they do as it is. Already we got too many." His eyes swept over Marcia.

"Who, me?" Doris straightened up indignantly.

"Shut up!" Valenti was losing his control. "If I tell you to wash dishes you'll wash dishes, sweep the floors and make a bed."

"I'm not much for dishes." Doris was doubtful. "I guess I'm more like the bed kind of a girl."

The huge figure of Booker loomed in the companionway. He ducked his head to enter.

"Is it all right if I go ashore with Michael, boss?'

"I don't know why we all can't go." Doris swung her long legs from the chair's arm. "I'm getting sick of this boat too. Besides"— she grinned wickedly at Booker— "the ape and I are both out of plutonium for our atomizer rayguns. What the hell would we do if there was an invasion from outer space?"

Marcia stood up. "I'm going ashore." She made the statement calmly but with a challenge.

For a moment Valenti glared at her. His teeth were partially bared in an animal snarl. Finally, he shrugged his shoulders indifferently.

"Go ahead. All of you. Get the hell away from me. I'll be glad to be alone for a while." He addressed Michael. "If they're not on the dock when you're ready to come back leave them there."

Doris jumped up, ducked her head to glance in a mirror, and then with a mock gesture of trustfulness offered her hand to Booker.

"Come on, buster. Maybe we can find a Mickey Mouse at the movies."

Walking down Main Street, all but deserted at this time of the evening, Patrick lifted his head, breathing deeply of the air which, even here, carried with it the scent of oleander.

"No wonder you like it," he marveled. "Yesterday I covered an assignment on a North River pier. There was slush to your ankles. Maybe we're both suckers to go back. There ought to be jobs on one of the sheets in Miami."

"I've been thinking about it," Jeff admitted.

"Not you, kid," Patrick scoffed. "Not you, or," he conceded a little sadly, "me either. We've been playing the big circuit too long."

As they entered the Fish Shack, Jeff knew he had made a mistake. It should have occurred to him that they might run into the judge here. Now, he could only hope that the lonely figure, hunched over an empty glass at the end of the dim bar, would mean nothing to Patrick. At the sound of the door opening and closing the judge looked up. His fogged eyes followed them as they took stools and then he nodded but did not speak.

Jeff took a seat on Patrick's right, his body partly screening the judge from the photographer. Apparently, the judge meant nothing to Patrick, who had settled himself happily and was reading aloud the legend. "The Fish Shack, Where You Get Fried." He shook his head with simulated admiration. "Now," he drawled, "that there is a real knee-slapper."

Bud took a lazy swipe at the bar with a damp rag. "What will it be, Mr. Martin? The same as usual?"

"Make it double, Bud." He indicated Patrick with a jerk of his head. "This is Mr. Patrick. If he ever comes in and mentions my name, wanting credit, don't give it to him. What's on the menu?"

Bud put out the bourbon and glasses. "That's one thing that don't never change, the menu, car-te de joor, like they say in French. Fried shrimp, chicken in a basket, steaks. Want to order now?"

The radio played softly and the little bar was dim and quietly peaceful. Bud was reading the sport section of a Miami paper and Patrick was pleasantly engaged in watering his bourbon. There was little chance, Jeff thought, of the photographer recognizing the judge and then, unaccountably, he was angry with himself. Damn it! How long did he think he could kid everyone, including himself? He had a job to do and the way to do it was to say to Patrick, "There, at the end of the bar, the old man is Judge Amos Cartright Get a shot of him just that way." The words wouldn't come.

"Young man." The vibrant richness of the voice pealed through the room. "I'll have a little more whiskey, and see what Mr. Martin and his friend will have."

Bud winked at Jeff and laid aside his paper. "Yes sir, Senator, right away!"

For a long moment Patrick stared at the bulking figure, the shaggy head and lifted face of the judge. Then slowly, thoughtfully he reached into his jacket pocket for a cigarette. He lit a match and over its flame his eyes were disconcertingly level as they held Jeff's uncomfortable gaze.

"You're a no-good bastard, Jeff." He spoke softly. "You were going to let it ride, weren't you?"

"Look, Jim." It was a weak protest. "Don't do it this way, not like a character shot of an old guy in a bar. Leave him something. Tomorrow we'll get him cleaned up and shaved. Remember who he was."

"I remember you were a good reporter once." He leaned down from the stool, opened the case and took out the Speed-Graphic with its flashlight attachment. Jeff watched him with an empty sensation of helplessness. Patrick was right. This was his profession, his obligation to the paper for which he worked. "Make an ass out of yourself if you want to." Patrick continued. "But I'm damned if you'll do it to me."

With a sensation that was close to nausea Jeff watched as Patrick made a quick adjustment to his camera, knowing that eventually he would back up the pictures with words from his typewriter. He glanced down the room. The judge's head was again half averted. Patrick sighted the camera while Bud regarded him with open-mouthed curiosity.

"Hey!" Patrick's shout was a report.

Startled, the judge instinctively lifted his head. There was the white, blinding flash of the bulb. It filled the room with a merciless light, illuminating the tired, disillusioned features.

"Thank you, Judge." Patrick spoke crisply, professionally. "Will you hold it for a minute." He behaved as though he actually believed Judge Cartright was going to pose willingly.

Slowly, painfully, the judge stood up. He swayed on his feet for a second, holding to the edge of the bar until he was steady. There was, Jeff thought with unconscious admiration, a great dignity in this man. It was something that shone through the lost and dissipated years. It was an innate majesty of spirit. He moved deliberately now toward them and the door and as he approached Patrick's camera went into action again. The judge, momentarily blinded by the flash, halted briefly and passed a tired and trembling hand over his eyes. Then his shoulders straightened.

"Somehow." The voice was controlled. "Somehow I didn't think you'd do it quite this way, Mr. Martin." He stood looking at them.

Even Patrick was not insensible to the rebuke. He pretended a quick absorption in the mechanism of the camera. Jeff felt his stomach turn over. In this moment the judge was a lion, proud but old, set upon by jackals. He stared fixedly at Patrick until the photographer was forced to look up.

"I would not think that you sleep very well at night, young man. But"— and Jeff could have sworn there was a sad smile behind the words—"neither do I." He inclined his head. "Good night, gentlemen."

Without speaking, Patrick put away the camera and then, swinging around on the stool, he swept up the bourbon bottle almost angrily, pouring until the drink slopped over. He did not look at Jeff. Bud, unable to account for what had happened, gazed with an inarticulate fascination from Jeff to the photographer.

"All right," Patrick growled. "Go ahead and say it."

Jeff shook his head. "What the hell is there to say? It's the job you were sent down to do, isn't it? Like the little whore said: I guess you're just lucky."

CHAPTER EIGHT

The figure, as it wove stumblingly across the grassy flats, seemed to be more that of a shambling, bewildered animal than a man. The arms dangled loosely, flapping against his sides as broken and disjointed members. The head was bowed, lolling with each step as the feet moved mechanically, driven by unreasoning terror.

There were no tears to cry; no sound to break the silence beyond that of labored, whistling gasps for air. Within Judge Amos Cartright there was nothing but the dull ache of humiliation and degradation. It filled his body and mind until there was room for nothing more. He stared ahead but did not see, no longer caring where his unsteady legs took him. There was only the compulsion to keep moving.

Once he halted, dimly aware that he had somehow crossed the marsh and moved upward upon a gentle slope with its tangled oaks, moss draped as grey skeletons, and scattered clumps of scrub palmetto. Later, he was vaguely aware of standing in the center of a broad highway as automobiles roared down upon him out of the night. The sky was filled with the rushing sound of demons and they descended to shriek at him with a cacophony of strident voices, their headlights veering wildly, their shouted imprecations torn from their mouths by the wind. As he halted there he had one lucid moment. This was the answer, to stand here until struck down. Then, unaccountably, he found himself moving forward. The feet slid forward with a volition of their own. He did not will it so.

There were fleeting impressions; the sharp fragrance of pine as he plodded along a ridge, bumping against the bronzed pillars of the high trees. There was the clinging sand of open country and the distant, melancholy call of a whippoorwill; a field into whose furrows he pitched headlong, lying there for what seemed an eternity before he could summon the strength to pull himself to his hands and knees. In these hours he was mortally stricken, a primitive man fleeing from his enemies, seeking only shelter, a cave, a tangle of brush, anything that would shield him from inquisitive eyes.

There was a yard and an old automobile tire hanging on a rope from the limb of a chinaberry tree to make a swing for children. There was the not too confident barking of a dog, an unpainted cabin and behind its window pane of oiled paper a light flickered. There was an old orange crate over which he fell with a crashing sound and later the concerned and apprehensive face of a Negro man, bending above him, holding a lantern high for light. There was a woman who joined him and they stared fearfully at each other. From far away the judge heard voices.

"This heah a white man."

"He drunk, Anson, or hurt bad ...."

On the Cay's main street, Doris, in shorts and silk blouse, her long, tanned legs gleaming with the color of polished mahogany, created a sensation that would be equaled only by the second coming. Flanked by Marcia, who seemed quakerish by comparison, she sauntered deliberately. Booker, bringing up the rear and towering above them, was almost unnoticed. The Cay's residents halted to stare, and even the young sports in front of Pellicier's Billiard Parlor were too astonished to whistle.

Where the light, spilling from the front of a Rexall Store, laid an oblong across the sidewalk, Doris paused and turned inquiringly to Marcia.

"Well, doll. We've seen it. Up one side of the street and down the other. What do we do now?"

Marcia grinned. "We might take our clothes off, but I don't think it would add anything to the effect."

"I thought there'd be a movie," Booker rumbled complainingly. He gazed longingly at the store's gleaming fountain. "How about a soda?" He brightened.

"With Scotch in it?" Doris ignored him, directing her question to Marcia.

"It'll get us under cover at least." Marcia nodded. "I think they're already alerting the vigilantes."

"I want to see a movie." Booker was not satisfied.

Marcia laid a soothing hand on his arm. "I've got some dirty French postcards you can look at when we get back to the boat."

"Aw! You're always kiddin'." Booker was sheepish. "You were kiddin' about your old lady bein' a hooker, too. I ain't so dumb."

"You couldn't be, Buster. You just couldn't be." Doris made a compliment of the statement. "Now, we'll just go and find a good saloon and you can play the pinball machine while doll and I lap it up."

Jeff and Patrick still sat at the bar, but there was little conversation between them and no one mentioned food. They drank slowly, reflectively, as troubled men will, and found no pleasure in the stuff. Bud had half a dozen customers to take care of and was busy at the other end of the bar. Patrick pushed away his drink.

"Hell. I'm going back to the hotel." He was angry with himself. The memory of Judge Cartright's face would not leave him. "You coming?" He swung around on the stool and the movement was arrested by the entrance of Doris, Marcia and Booker. He whistled softly. Sentences were broken off by the spectacular appearance of the trio.

Doris, through a process of cerebration understood only by herself, had decided on the *grande dame* manner for the Fish Shack. Her glance traveled over Patrick and the others and a faint wrinkling of the nose indicated that a bad odor had assailed it. Figuratively, she lifted patrician skirts, sweeping regally through a particularly noisome sewer. When she was settled on a stool she crooked a finger at the awestruck Bud.

"Booze. Scotch booze." She relaxed then and gazed dreamily at Bud. "Close your mouth, junior. Your tonsils show. Booze for the ladies and a root beer for Mr. Booker."

As in a trance Bud placed a bottle of Scotch, glasses and water on the bar. He stared hungrily at Doris and made an effort to speak, but his Adam's apple bobbed futilely and no sound came.

Drink in hand and with her little finger extended stiffly Doris permitted her glance to roam along the mirror reflecting the bar's patrons. Her gaze rested for a second on Jeff, passed disdainfully on and then snapped back. A frown ridged her forehead. She took a swallow of the drink, peered at the glass and then lifted her eyes to regard Jeff again.

"I know you." She spoke to his image in the mirror. "From where do I know you?"

"Polly Adler's?" Jeff was pleasantly attentive.

Marcia smiled faintly to herself. She, also, studied Jeff and the man beside him. Her scrutiny was cool, speculative, as she weighed their presence in connection with Doris's statement. It probably meant nothing. Doris must know a lot of men. This one being here had no relation to Valenti's arrival. But, the word was out. Who knew where it would reach. She swirled the ice within the glass.

"You're that cop!" Doris's exclamation was triumphant. "Or if you're not a cop you came aboard with one at Palm Beach."

At the word cop Booker turned from an absorbed interest in tilting the pinball machine with one finger. His head thrust forward turtlelike and then he shuffled over to stand accusingly before Jeff and Patrick.

"You followin' us, huh?" The hands swung restlessly at his sides. "What you followin' us for? You come on the boat in Palm Beach an' now you're here; it looks like we're bein' followed. So tell me why?"

Jeff turned on his stool, looking up into Booker's glowering face. He was irritated by this senseless belligerency and idiot mouthing. "Go away. Go off in a corner and tear some telephone books in half."

"You want I should handle him for you, Dorrie? You want I should, huh?" Booker was anxious to display an accomplishment, waiting to be asked to perform.

"Sit down, Booker." Marcia's command was sharply impatient.

"Who're you, huh?" Booker, unable to cope with more than one situation at a time, turned upon the girl. His eyes were hot pink marbles. "Who you givin' orders to? I never seen you before. Just a snotty dame. You keep out of this. I take care of Dorrie, see?"

Every head was turned, every ear strained to listen. Bud leaned anxiously across the bar, a tremulous, placating smile appearing timidly. "Look, folks, let's don't have any trouble. Now, you all have a drink on the house. Mr. Martin was just sittin' here."

"We're not going to have any trouble, Bud." Jeff was quietly reassuring.

"Your friend a cop, too?" Doris persisted.

"Look, sister." Jeff was bored, patient. "Why don't you just have your drink? I'm not a cop, if that's what bothers you. Now, put your gorilla on a stool and feed him some peanuts." He took a glassine sack from a small rack on the bar and tossed it to her. "We'll keep it quiet and friendly, the way it was." He turned to his unfinished drink.

There was an outraged bellow. "Who you callin' a gorilla?" Booker's hand clamped on Jeff's shoulder, whirling him about. "From Dorrie it don't sound bad, like when she says ape, but I don't take it from no one else."

Jeff jerked his shoulder away. He wasn't underestimating the stupid fury of the man facing him. Booker swayed menacingly, his hands opening and closing convulsively. He moved closer, thrusting himself against Jeff, looming above him. There was a soft scraping of stools along the bar and several men sidled out quickly to stand on the sidewalk.

"You about ready, Scoop?" Patrick's question was casual.

Jeff laughed softly. "Why, friend, I guess this is as good a time as any. Should we go?"

He stood up quickly and his knee lifted with the drive of a piston, catching the surprised Booker full in the crotch. Jeff felt the bony cap stab into the man and heard his scream of agony. As he bent in torment Jeff's hand sliced across his throat, the rigid edge cutting off the cry, crushing it into a strangled bubble that clotted and choked. At his side Patrick had risen, grasping the half-filled bottle of bourbon at the neck. He brought it down almost indifferently upon Booker's bowed head.

Booker fell with a heaviness that shook the room and rattled the glasses on their shelves. He rolled once and came to rest, face down and with his open mouth pressed against the floor. It had all happened so quickly that it seemed not to have happened at all and for the moment there was a complete and stunned silence.

Patrick looked at the unbroken bottle approvingly and then replaced it on the bar.

He winked at Jeff. "I guess they must be making bourbon stronger these days."

Bud stretched on tiptoe to stare at the unconscious figure on the floor. "Jesus! Mr. Martin." He breathed. "Is he dead, you think? Should I get the marshal, or maybe a doctor?"

Booker moaned and began to retch, slobbering and thrusting his face into the filth. He whimpered and then sobbed, pulling his legs up against his belly, hands pressing down upon his crotch in an effort to hold away the pain.

"You're real tough, aren't you?" Doris lit a cigarette and snapped the burnt match in Jeff's direction. She eyed the tortured Booker indifferently.

"Why don't you keep him on a chain?" Jeff caught the match.

"The ape isn't going to be happy with you when he comes to." There was a malicious smile behind the words. "He's got a little brain but a big memory. If I were you I'd take a trip."

"And if I were you I'd take him back to your friend Valenti. I thought he wanted everything nice and quiet. How is he, by the way?"

Marcia stood up. "Let's get out of here." She regarded the sprawled Booker with distaste. "What are we going to do with him?"

Doris slid from her stool and poked with the toe of her sandal at Booker's ribs. "Get up, ape," she commanded.

Booker, coughing, pulled himself to hands and knees. He turned his head, looking up with a dull, uncomprehending stare. There was no fight in him, only the hot flame that seared his crotch. With painful effort he hauled himself upright and then staggered toward the door, lurching into it with a crash and almost falling headlong to the sidewalk beyond.

Doris nodded to Marcia. "Come on, doll, unless you want to stick around for the second feature." She addressed Jeff almost affably. "I'll tell Valenti you were asking for him. He'll be interested."

As the door closed behind the girls the room was suddenly filled with sound as those who had remained all began to talk at once.

Patrick smiled at Jeff. "Somehow, I feel better. I might even eat one of those steaks. How about it, Bud?"

"Yeah! Sure. Comin' right up." Bud was still unnerved by what had happened. He looked at Jeff with a new respect. "I sure never figured you could take him, Mr. Martin."

"I had a little help." Jeff grinned at Patrick. "Put a steak on for me too."

When they were settled in one of the booths, Patrick turned to Jeff. "Do you know who she is? Not the blonde, I mean?"

"No."

"Her name used to be Harper. Her brother went to the pokey for a part in an armored car holdup in Brooklyn. She was married to a thief in L.A. by the name of Blake. So." He whistled softly. "Tell me what's she doing in a bar down here with Valenti's muff and Valenti, too? This could get real interesting, Scoop."

As from a great distance Jeff heard the persistent knocking on his door. It nagged at him, finally driving off sleep. Then he heard Judy's voice and in it a pleading note of desperation. He snapped upright, wide awake, and swung his legs over the side of the bed. Fumbling at the wall, he found the switch and the room was flooded with a harsh light from the uncovered, overhead bulbs. He unbolted and opened the door.

"Judy, honey. What's wrong?"

He drew her inside, saw the fear in her eyes, felt her body quiver and understood she was on the verge of tears. Holding her with one arm he pushed the door shut with his free hand.

"Now, take it easy." He tried to soothe her. "Tell me what's happened."

"It's Pop." Her eyes were deeply shadowed with concern. "I waited and waited and he didn't come home. Then, I guess, I slept for a little while. I don't know. But Jeff," she was pleading for some assurance, "every place is closed now. I know he was drinking but there is no place for him to drink at this hour and he still hasn't come home."

Jeff glanced at his watch. It was after three. "Honey, nothing could happen to him here in the Cay. We'll find him. Stop worrying." He touched her cheek gently, wiping away a trace of a tear.

"But I've been every place." She wasn't satisfied. "I even went to Bud's and woke him up. He said Pop had been in earlier in the evening." She drew away, staring at him uncomprehendingly. "He said you and another man were there and that the man with you had taken some pictures of Pop. What is it, Jeff? What is it you know and won't tell me? Why would anyone want to take his picture and in a bar when he had been drinking?"

Silently Jeff cursed Bud and then realized the boy wasn't to blame. What he had told Judy was unusual enough to excite her curiosity. He would tell her about it.

"Let's see if we can find him first." He led her to a chair. "I'll get some clothes on. We can talk later."

She sat, staring down at locked hands, while he put on slacks, shirt and thrust his feet into a pair of sneakers in the bathroom. When he came out her eyes followed him. The expression of apprehension was gone, replaced by a perplexed groping for an answer. There was doubt and even a wary suspicion in her gaze.

"I told you. I have looked every place." The words were dulled by weariness.

He took her hands, drawing her up. She came reluctantly. "Be reasonable, baby." He attempted to make the request light. "You couldn't have looked every place or you would have found him. He didn't just vanish in a puff of smoke. If he was drinking a lot then he must have passed out. I mean," he corrected himself hastily, "he must have gone to sleep somewhere."

She shook her head. "Not Pop. I know him. Someone always puts him in a taxi or he gets one for himself. Then he comes home. He always comes home. Something happened tonight. Something happened that made him not want to come home. There's a reason, Jeff, and you know what it is."

He took the keys to the rented convertible from the bureau, standing with his back to her, unwilling to face the indictment in her eyes. Finally he turned slowly and nodded.

"Let's find him first, Judy. I think it's something he would want to tell you himself. Believe me, it will be better if he does. I think that's the way he wants it." His hands went to her shoulders, drawing her close and bending to kiss her tenderly. Her lips were cold, unresponsive, her gaze fixed upon him. "Come on now." He led her to the door and she followed like a bewildered and lost child ....

Mr. Hathaway had been awakened by the knocking on the adjoining room's door, heard the persistent calling of a girl's voice and noted its urgency and fear. Because he was a methodical man he turned on the light and noted the time. He lay, now, arms locked behind his head, staring at the ceiling, listening to footsteps on the creaking boards of the uncarpeted hallway.

Without much apparent effort Mr. Hathaway had learned a great many things within the span of a few hours since his arrival in Redemption Cay. From the loquacious proprietor he heard that the man in the room next to his was a reporter from New York. He had, also, been in the lobby when Jim Patrick checked in and noted the photographer's case slung over his shoulder. From the end of Norn's dock he had seen the *Oriole II* swinging at anchor in deep water; had watched with pleased interest as the dinghy, carrying the two girls, Spain and Booker came into the landing. Later, he had been idling along Main Street when Booker, stunned and all but helpless, half fell through the Fish Shack's door.

The presence of a reporter and a photographer in the Cay disturbed him. The very fact that they were here indicated something beyond mere chance. There had to be a reason and Mr. Hathaway didn't know what it was. They threatened all sorts of unexpected contingencies. Mr. Hathaway wanted things to proceed smoothly and a reporter asking questions, a photographer taking pictures, were not calculated to maintain the delicate balance of a precarious situation. Valenti must be allowed to pursue his way without interference. Left alone, certain things would move into their proper places as chessmen guided by an invisible hand. He wanted no unexpected checkmate. When the hallway was quiet again he turned out the light but it was a long time before he fell into a troubled sleep.

Main Street was a long tunnel of darkness as Jeff turned the car into it from the hotel's parking space. Single bulbs in the bank, the drug store and the A&P glowed dimly. They were the only persons abroad at this hour. Judy was hunched into a corner of the seat, her body turned as she studied his face.

"Do you think he would go down around the docks?"

"He wouldn't go anyplace but home." The reply was toneless.

"This time he did." Unaccountably he found himself growing angry and the words were sharp. Then he relented and was contrite. "I'm sorry." He reached to place his hand over hers and felt it draw slowly away.

On the shell road skirting the river he swung the car from side to side, permitting the headlights to sweep over the edges and once he stopped, got out and peered inside a boat that had been drawn up for painting. Returning, settling behind the wheel without comment, he drove out toward the marsh, wishing the car had a spotlight. This was a futile search and he knew it. The old man could be lying drunk almost anywhere. They could pass him a dozen times in the dark and never know it. In his heart, though, he knew Judge Cartright would not be found here. When he had left the Fish Shack he was a haunted man, unwilling to face himself or Judy. That was why he had not gone home.

In the level, cleared space, beyond which ran the canal where the houseboat was moored, he again stopped the car. This time he walked through the waist-high reeds, feeling the spongy earth beneath his feet. Judy did not attempt to follow. It was as though she, also, knew the judge was not here.

"If he came this far," she called to him, "he would have come the rest of the way."

Jeff returned to stand beside her door. He lit a cigarette, offered it to her. She shook her head.

"Judy. Judy, listen to me." He was pleading, made miserable by her quiet resignation. "There's not much more we can do until it gets light. If he's sleeping it off somewhere we could pass and repass him. You know that."

"Yes. I know." Her voice was small. She turned the door's handle, swinging it open and sliding out. "I'll—I'll make some coffee. Will you wait with me? I'm afraid to be alone."

A lamp in the cabin guided them across the plank gangway. He sat on the edge of a bunk while she busied herself in the corner galley with a coffee pot.

"I want you to tell me, Jeff." She kept her back to him, pretending a concentration on the butane flame. "I have to know."

He sighed. "I suppose so. It's a long story, Judy. Some of it I don't know, part is only guessing."

"We have plenty of time until daylight." She still didn't turn to look at him.

When the coffee was ready they took their cups outside, both recognizing that what was to be said might better be told within the enshrouding darkness. They sat on the deck and he put his arm around her. This time she did not pull away but seemed to creep within the shelter with a tiny whimper.

"You know I love you."

"I—I hoped you did, Jeff."

"It isn't something I've said before. Maybe that's why it has taken me so long to say it now." He took a deep breath. "You must know I wouldn't hurt you. Let me talk, don't answer, don't ask any questions until I have finished. I want you to believe that a lot of what has happened was only an accident. I came here for a vacation, nothing more. Then, because a man was released from prison six thousand miles away, a whole chain of events began to link up. Once it started I couldn't stop it. It was like a bunch of firecrackers, one setting off another." He took a swallow of the coffee and lit another cigarette. Then he started to talk and the things he said had their beginning in a hot street in Brooklyn, a man with a pushcart and an armored truck with over a million dollars in it. When he came to Valenti and Judge Amos Cartright she started, turning to stare unbelievingly.

"That's why you called him Judge?"

"Yes."

He told her everything he knew then, told it as carefully as he would have written it.

"I'm not sure what the connection is." He concluded. "There may be none beyond the fact that Judge Cartright sentenced Valenti and Valenti has been looking for something. He's aboard the *Oriole II*."

Her arms were wrapped about her knees and she stared out over the marsh. When she finally spoke her words were almost inaudible. "I have always felt there was something. Pop never told me. When I was small I used to ask where I was born, where my mother was. He'd pretend it was a game, saying the fairies left me on the doorstep. Later, when I was a lot older, I stopped asking because I understood he didn't want to talk about it." She looked again into his face. "Who was my mother, Jeff?"

He told her, dreading the inevitable query.

"But Pop. He—he isn't my father, is he?"

"I don't know, Judy. I only know what Burrows told me. He said it had been a childless marriage. The judge will have to tell you now." He felt exhausted.

"And tonight, in the Fish Shack, what Bud said about a photographer? He's from your paper, isn't he? You sent for him?"

"I didn't send for him, Judy. You have to believe that. He came down on orders from the desk. I've been stalling this thing for days. You must understand. Otherwise, I would have had the story on the wire five minutes after I learned who the judge really was."

"But you're going to write it?" There was an icy calm behind the question.

"Yes." He replied miserably. "Yes, Judy. I'm going to write it. Don't you see I have no choice?"

"I don't know, Jeff." She stood up, turned to face the river, her arms crossed upon the rail. When he moved to join her she shook her head. "Don't touch me now, Jeff. I'm a little dead inside, as dead as Judge Amos Cartright will be after you and your paper have finished with him." She wheeled to face him and her cry was one of agony. "Why couldn't you have let him—us—alone?"

"You're blaming me for something that isn't my fault, and you don't or won't understand."

"I understand you are hounding an old man, a heartsick, broken man who wanted only to live here in peace. He was happy. We were happy. Maybe not all the time but this was what he wanted. Doesn't it make you sick to know what you are doing?"

"The judge wasn't happy. A man doesn't drink as he does if he's happy. He was only trying to run away, pull a blanket over his head, crawl back into the womb. Whatever his reasons for disappearing they haven't been enough. What he did has eaten at him like a cancer."

Stubbornly she shook her head. "What are you offering him, a forced return to something from which he wanted to escape? Don't try and rationalize it. To you he's so many lines of type, so many columns and pictures. I think I despise you. You make me crawl inside." She was trembling uncontrollably. "Let me alone. Go away, Jeff. I'll find Pop somewhere. I don't want you any more."

CHAPTER NINE

Deputy Sheriff Bill Longworth took the call, glanced ruefully at the clock, made a note on a pad and hung up. He reached for his hat and strode unhurriedly to his car. The world was filled with drunks and he seemed to get them all. Fifteen minutes more and Payton would have been on duty.

As his car flashed along the empty highway he turned on the commercial radio and listened to an all-night disk jockey as the miles slipped beneath his wheels. Twenty minutes later he turned into a filling station.

"You the man who called the sheriff's office?" He asked the sleepy-eyed attendant.

"Yeah, Sheriff." He jerked a thumb across his shoulder. "He's over there." The voice lifted in a call. "Hey! You boy. Come here."

A form separated itself from the gloom beyond the frame of lights and the Negro came forward hesitantly. He touched his hat respectfully and stood waiting, for this was the law and a man approached it with caution.

"You the one who called in?" Longworth's words were softly spoken and reassuring.

"Yes suh. Oah," the amendment was quickly made, "this gint'm'n did hit foah me." He nodded toward the station operator.

"Well, get in and we'll have a look."

They traveled a back road, unpaved and little more than two deep ruts gouged out of the sand and snaking unpredictably through the pine woods.

"Hit raight ovah theah." The Negro spoke ten minutes later and indicated the small blob of yellow light in a cabin.

Inside, Longworth bent over the still unconscious form of Judge Amos Cartright. He listened to the uncertain breathing, smelled the sour reek of whiskey, noted the blotched and unhealthy pallor. Then he went outside, called the dispatcher and requested an ambulance. He returned to search through the judge's pockets for some identification and found nothing but a few crumpled bills.

"Do you know him? Does he live around here?"

The Negro shook his head. "Nevah seen 'im, Capt'n, suh." He turned to his wife, who stood with her back pressed against the far wall ef the room. "You know th' man, Delcey?"

"No." The reply was a whisper.

Longworth made a few notes in a book and then went outside, sitting on the edge of the porch, waiting for the ambulance. When it finally arrived he stood by until the man was carried on a stretcher and slid inside and then went to his car. The Negro was standing nearby. He came over.

"Theah ain' no trouble foah Delcey an' me, is theah, Capt'n, suh? Hit was liak I say. He jus' come an' frammed into an' ol' crate, fallin' on his face."

"No. It's all right. I believe you. If he dies, though, you'll have to come in and make a statement."

He drove away, thinking a little unhappily of the Negro's innate suspicion of the law. They never thought of it as something to help them but only another form of the whites' persecution. Never, as long as he could remember, had a Negro voluntarily turned to the law for assistance where only his own kind was involved.

The sun was breaking through an early morning overcast when, on an impulse, he turned from the highway to follow the road into Redemption Cay. He was off duty now and hungry. That newspaper fellow, Martin, might still be around. There had been a spontaneous understanding between them at that first meeting; he'd like to see him again.

With the arrival of daylight Jeff had retraced the area of search he and Judy had covered during the night and extended it to include the docks and a few side streets. He was tired now, unshaven and heartsick. As he climbed the hotel's steps the sound of a car in the driveway caused him to turn.

Longworth lifted a hand in a half salute. "I didn't know there was anything in the Cay to keep a man up all night." He trotted up the steps and they shook hands. "I wondered if you were still here. Had breakfast?"

"No. I'll have some coffee with you. What brings you down here?"

"I had a job out in the backwoods." They talked as they went into the dining room.

They took a table near the windows and Longworth glanced out, his eyes covering the sweep of the river. He looked at Jeff with surprise.

"Isn't that the McElroy boat out there?"

"It came in last night."

"Valenti still aboard?"

"I guess so. I haven't seen him." He smiled. "Your blonde dish has been joined by another one who's quite a dish herself. They were on the town last night with the crew-cut boy." He hesitated and then leaned his arms on the table. "I need your help."

"Personal or official?"

"A little of both, maybe." Then, for the third time within twelve hours he went over the story of Judge Cartright. As he talked all trace of easy banter left Longworth. He was interested, attentive and quietly absorbed. "I still think I'm right." Jeff concluded. "It's got to tie in. I'm not playing detective. I'm still a reporter ... or maybe I'm not."

"Where is Cartright now?"

"The damn fool has disappeared. That's what kept me up all night."

Longworth took a swallow of coffee and forked up some of the scrambled eggs and bacon the waiter had placed before them. He chewed meditatively for a moment.

"Big man? Sixty, sixty-five? Shaggy hair and a fine face that has gone to pieces?"

Jeff was surprised. "How did you know?"

"He kept me up all night too. I've got him in the County Hospital. We'll put in a call and find out how he is. The intern diagnosed it as acute alcoholism and exhaustion."

A wave of relief flooded over Jeff. If anything had happened to the judge he would never have been able to face Judy or convince her that he wasn't responsible for driving him to an act of desperation.

He stood up. "I've got to tell Judy. The kid's out of her mind, and it's partly my fault."

Longworth waved his fork negligently. "We can do better than that. We'll take her to the hospital if you'll let me finish my breakfast." The smile that was diffident, almost shy at times, appeared in sketched lines about the eyes. "After all, I'm not in love; just hungry." He continued to eat.

Jeff sank back in the chair. "I suppose I am the frantic lover, wearing it on my sleeve. I've known a lot of girls but this one really got to me where it hurts."

"Worse things could happen to a man." The deputy finished his eggs and bacon, gulped the last swallow of coffee and arose.

On the way out they were met by Mr. Hathaway, who seemed to bounce on the tips of his toes, filled with a high good humor for what the day might hold. His eyes brightened at the sight of the deputy.

"Sheriff Longworth! Now! This is a surprise. I'm delighted to see you again." He cocked his head. "What brings you to this peaceful little spot? Not constabulary duty, I hope. It is difficult to think of malefactors here or that the world is beset by evildo-ers." He winked at Longworth as though they shared a humorous secret.

"How are you, Mr. Hathaway?" Longworth introduced Jeff.

"Oh! My! I already know Mr. Martin by sight and reputa-tion." He chuckled delightedly. "Somehow, I feel we have a com-mon interest here; very common, if I may make a bad pun." He fairly chortled at the blank expression on Jeff's face and then stepped to one side. "You were walking like men in a hurry, so I shan't detain you. Good-by, Sheriff. May I say that I find your presence, temporary though it may be, very reassuring? Very reassuring indeed."

"Who the hell is that?" Jeff was mystified. They strode through the lobby and outside to Longworth's car.

The deputy laughed quietly. "I asked the same question the first time I ran into him. I'll tell you about it on the way to pick up your girl."

Judy, alone in the car's back seat, a small overnight bag beside her, kept her face turned to the open windows, staring unsee-ingly as the countryside flashed past. Jeff sat with Longworth, uncomfortable and unable to make small talk which might have relieved the tension. Save for one fleeting moment, when a gasp and her eyes betrayed her relief, Judy had maintained a wooden passiveness. Her silence was an accusation. Even Longworth felt the constraint and contented himself with a tuneless whistle and attention to the road. Not until they were at the hospital and Judy tried to open the door did he speak.

"They don't open from the inside, Miss Carter." He smiled at her. "If they did we'd have prisoners jumping out every time we slowed down." He came around to help her, taking the bag.

"Thank you." Judy spoke only to the deputy. "Thank you for everything; finding him, bringing him here." Her voice almost broke. "I'll be all right now. I'll go to a motel or somewhere until he is well enough to come home."

Jeff stood in unhappy silence as she ran up the steps and disappeared inside the building. Then he sighed and shook his head, returning to his place in the front seat. Not a word. Thank you. Go to hell. Nothing.

"You look like you could use some sleep." Longworth glanced at him. "It's too early for drinking. I don't feel like fishing. You're lousy company so I think I'll go back to Palm Beach. Call me if I can do anything."

"Thanks." Jeff nodded. "I'm in a hell of a spot. You can see that. I can lose my job or my girl, probably both." Abruptly his thoughts strayed. "Got any idea why that little insurance investigator is down here?"

The deputy was silent for a moment. "Yeah," he finally admitted. "I've got some ideas. They probably aren't much different from yours. When the time comes maybe we'll put them together."

Longworth left him at the hotel and he walked upstairs. There was a note from Patrick under the door. He didn't even bother to read it. To hell with him and to hell with Burrows. Despite Longworth's remark about the hour he poured himself a big drink and then, too tired to take a bath or undress, he fell into the bed and waited for the liquor to bring him sleep....

The shingled, single-storied house had grown grey and weathered with the years. It sprawled itself between the high sand-dunes as a contented beachcomber enjoying the sun and the soft, southeast wind. A broad screened porch opened to the ocean and the strip of soft beach. No light or telephone wires intruded and the sloping roof was bare of television antenna, shutting away the world outside. Although little more than a couple of waterway miles separated it from the mainland, the location was as secluded and remote as one of the tiny dots of land in the Philippine Archipelago.

In the living room, running the width of the house and sparsely furnished with chairs, couches and tables of bamboo and rattan, Michael Spain stood, gazing out of the window. Behind him Valenti lay upon his back on one of the couches, a hand covering his eyes as though to shade them from the sun or to force a concentration of thought. Doris, feet apart, fists on her hips, surveyed the unpacked luggage, the frayed curtains and rickety furniture.

"Boy! Is this a winter wonderland! Paradise enow. I read that in a poem, all about a guy getting himself potted underneath a tree." No one paid the slightest attention to her words. "What do we do now?" She demanded. "Make like Robinson Caruso?"

Valenti lifted his hand and stared at her from beneath drooping lids. A screen door at the back of the house slammed and they could hear Booker's grunt as he set down another load of the groceries Spain had brought over from the Cay.

"Dorrie?" Booker's yell bounced through the house. "What do you want to do with this stuff?"

"I know what you can do with it, Buster," she yelled back cheerfully.

"Go and help him," Valenti whispered. "Get that Lewis dame out of her room. What the hell. Does she think she's a guest? Maybe between the two of you you've got brains enough to fix some lunch." He sagged back against the cushions again.

"You mean all this and eating too?" Doris was astounded. "Am I glad I came!"

This time Valenti did not lift his hand. "I'm going to beat the hell out of you, Dorrie." He spoke wearily. "I'm going to kick you right in the guts it you don't shut up. Now, get out of here and do as I told you."

Doris studied him for a moment. "Yeah," she admitted finally. "I guess you would at that." On her way to the kitchen she rapped on a bedroom door. "Company in the parlor, doll," she sang out. "Get on your marabou and black lace stockings."

Spain had not moved from his place by the window nor did he turn when Valenti spoke.

"You'll go back into town this evening, Michael. Take Hal with you."

"I don't know. I could have been mistaken. It's almost too easy, too lucky. But," he frowned, "there was something about him I remembered when he staggered out of that bar. You know how he used to throw back his head? The face, too; older and tireder, but the eyes, yes, the eyes. They haven't changed much. I didn't want to ask any questions."

"You make sure, Michael." Valenti coughed with an empty sound. "You make sure and then bring him here. I have waited a long time. Too many years, Michael. There aren't so many left."

"When I'm sure, I'll bring him."

"Yes, Michael. Be sure. It's too late for mistakes. I feel like a very old man today. Do you know what I used to dream of Michael? At night, in that cell, I used to fill it with beautiful girls like Doris. They came right through the walls without any clothes on; wonderful, sleek girls with long legs and hard breasts like Dorrie. They were all over me. We'd drink fine wine, old brandy and they'd feed me from a hundred different dishes and then we'd make love in a pool of milky, perfumed hot water. And now," the words were the thin pipings of an old man made querulous by time, "when I eat I get indigestion and Doris only irritates me. Maybe it will be different, but find him, Michael, find him and bring him to me."

In one of Norn's flat-bottomed boats with outboard motor Mr. Hathaway bared a thin and milk-white chest to the sun, fancying he was drawing immeasurable benefits from its rays. He hummed contentedly to himself, trying to fit the tune to the perky explosions of the motor. In the bottom of the boat lay a fishing rod, and forward there was a live-bait bucket. Mr. Hathaway hadn't even bothered to examine them.

A few minutes ago he had passed the *Oriole II;* watching first as she emerged from the snaky length of the creek and, later waving cheerily to a figure at the wheel. The cruiser had dropped its speed as it drew upon him but once past, when its wake could no longer endanger the small craft, the bow had lifted with a surge of power. Mr. Hathaway was appreciative of this courtesy. It seemed to him that men who operated or lived aboard boats were better mannered than those found ashore. He wondered why.

As he entered a winding branch of the river he noted a directional marker and a sign: "Blackfish Creek." It had a nice, piratical sound and, somehow, seemed appropriate to the business at hand. The creek ran between solid banks of mangrove and now and then the noise of the motor tossed up startled flights of cranes nesting there. Beyond this there was no sound, no movement.

It had not been difficult to trace the *Oriole II* from Redemption Cay. Mr. Hathaway had gone to the only real estate agent in town and made innocent and not too interested inquiries about renting a house or a cottage on the beach.

"Now." The man had been mystified. "This here is a real funny thing. A fella come to my house last night, wanted to rent a house. Off a boat he was. Said it had to be quiet, seems like there's an invalid in the party. I rented him the old Abercrombie place up Blackfish Creek." He cackled. "It's sure God-quiet there. Fella took it without dickering. Now you come along. It's almost like we was getting set for another real Florida boom, although I really can't say I'd like to see that happen again."

Mr. Hathaway had not committed himself. He thanked the man and said he'd think it over. With the name Blackfish Creek in mind he went to Norn's and rented a boat and tackle.

"You sure you know how to handle a boat?" Norn had been skeptical.

"Oh! My yes. I was once a counselor at a boy's lake camp. I became quite expert."

"That must have been a hell of a long time ago," Norn commented sourly. "Just keep away from the inlet. There ain't no fish there anyhow. Fish the cricks. You might get some little snapper. Hell. They's a million fish an' a hundred cricks. Put 'em all together and you'd get quite a mess for supper." He snickered at his humor. "Just don't go gettin' lost. I ain't got no time to come huntin' for you."

"I'll be careful." Mr. Hathaway was reassuring. "I'll just mosey around. It really doesn't make any difference if I catch fish or not."

He had cruised around, not sure of his destination, venturing into shallow creeks, searching for something that would point the way to Blackfish Creek. Then he had seen the *Oriole II* and knew he had located what he wanted. Now, as he rounded a sweeping bend in the waterway he could see a straggling dock in the distance. It was too far away for him to identify the figures on the canted pier, but he knew who they were. He let go the tiller and hugged himself with an unconscious gesture of excitement.

On the dock Doris shaded her eyes and peered down the length of creek shimmering in the sunlight. Beside her Booker waited, the short necks of two five-gallon water bottles swinging easily from his hands.

"The boss wants some lunch, Dorrie. What you goin' to do about it?"

"Open a can." She had her eyes on the approaching boat. "He ain't a bad guy. It's like somethin's on his mind right now, though."

"Well. It isn't me. I. However the hell you say it."

Doris laughed to herself. She was, she thought, getting like the joke about the miner who took an old, toothless hag with him into the mountains. When she began to look good to him he knew it was time to come out. In a curious way, as someone might develop a fondness for a hippopotamus, Doris had reached the point of almost liking Booker. He was a lug, big, dumb, stupid and the target for her jibes, but he was a faithful dog, worshipping her with the slow, ponderous workings of a childlike mind. He wasn't a guy she would like to go to bed with. He wasn't a guy she would like to do anything with. But she could slap him on the rump like he was an ox. He waited on her, fetching and carrying. He was usually good for a laugh and Doris was discovering she needed to laugh. This business with Valenti was raveling at her nerves. The old man, she had decided, was some sort of a queer. He'd get in bed and do nothing; just lie there with his knees drawn up, shivering against her stomach like she was a hot water bottle or something. That really makes me a bag, she thought and snickered to herself. Valenti didn't need a girl and most of the time paid no attention to her. She wondered why he had brought her along and at the money he was paying for something he didn't use. This damn trip was giving her the creeps.

As Booker walked away toward the house carrying the water she caught herself thinking about the two guys last night who had belted him in that bar. That was what she needed, someone with life in him. The one who took Booker, the fellow who had come aboard in Palm Beach with the cop. Right now she could use him. The idea stimulated her and she pressed the palms of her hands against her breasts and then took a deep breath. She lit a cigarette and sat atop one of the dock's pilings. This would not be a bad place with a guy like that. They'd lie around naked in the hot sun on the beach. In the evening they could open a jug and get a little fractured. Hell. She wouldn't even mind getting breakfast. Boy. She marveled. I'm sure getting twitchy. I'm even thinking of giving it away. How do you like that? But, who the hell am I going to give it to? Nobody even asks. Isn't that something?

She turned her head at the sound of a step on the dock's loose planking. Marcia came toward her. A real, cool muff, Doris thought, but I can't figure her out. What the hell is she doing in this charade? The doll was as cold and as hard as a pimp's hand on your mouth. She had Valenti bluffed, or near it. She spit in his eyes every time she spoke and didn't seem to give a damn that he was supposed to be the big spoke. Funny part of it was the old man took it. Doris wondered why.

"Hi, duchess." Doris indicated another piling and motioned down the creek and to the approaching boat. "Make like it's the Norfolk Yard and we're waiting for the fleet to come in."

Marcia stood, gazing at the boat. It was a quarter of a mile away and the sound of the single-cylindered motor was startlingly clear in the silence.

"Mike Spain says to get some lunch ready. Want to help?"

"Mike Spain is a pain in the ass." Doris was unimpressed. "As a matter of fact this whole cruise hurts me in the same place. I can't figure why you ever signed up."

"I had my reasons. Got a cigarette?"

Doris tossed her a package and a book of matches. "I thought so too when Spain gave me the word. You know, a lot of people still remember Valenti so I figured it for glamor, big hotel suite in Miami, night clubs, race track, hot shots and a lot of muscle to keep the squares away. So what? I might as well have brought a pair of coveralls. I haven't even been laid yet and I figured that would be the first thing he wanted after fifteen years in the trap. Maybe it's really like they say. They feed them saltpeter." She grinned suddenly. "That always sounded like a dirty word to me."

Marcia laughed with quiet amusement but her eyes were fixed on the approaching boat. She could make out a single occupant and there was something vaguely familiar about him.

In his boat, Mr. Hathaway had come to a decision. Man, he told himself, is frequently a rational and reasonable animal. Under proper conditions, if certain facts were put before him with logic, he would accept them. He, Roland Hathaway, thought the time had come to test this theory. Valenti was a free man now. The years of prison were behind him and he would certainly have no wish to return. It should be explained to Mr. Valenti that he could remain free for just as long as he put no hand on the money he sought. Once he touched it he was again a felon and as such Mr. Hathaway was firmly determined that he go to jail. It was just possible, he argued to himself, Valenti might accept this inescapable fact. Naturally, he would squirm and protest violently. He was a man of evil intent and purpose but Mr. Hathaway had logic on his side. If Valenti would accept it, everyone would be saved a great deal of unnecessary trouble and needless skirmishing. He angled the boat toward the dock.

Doris, her legs twined about the piling, gave interested attention to the boat's approach. "He's pretty old and skinny to be a sailor," she said to Marcia over her shoulder.

Mr. Hathaway cut the motor and allowed the craft to drift. Once alongside the dock he looked up.

"Miss Lewis." He nodded pleasantly. "We do seem to encounter each other in the most astonishing fashion. Never again shall I limit the probability of coincidence."

"How do you do, Mr. Hathaway."

Doris was surprised. "You know?"

"I know." Marcia was short.

"Well." Doris sighed. "He sure isn't Vic Mature, but what can you expect on a desert island?"

"Is there a ladder or something?" Mr. Hathaway estimated the distance separating him from the dock's level.

"Do you want to come ashore, Mr. Hathaway?" Marcia could not keep the surprise from her tone.

"Oh! My yes! That is what I really came for, to come ashore and have a chat with Mr. Valenti. It is just possible we may avoid any number of unpleasant situations. Oh! Yes. I really think now I should have a talk with him."

Marcia shrugged indifferently. "There's a landing float back there." She pointed to the shore end of the dock, where Michael had moored his rented boat. "Tie up there. But you're being a fool, Mr. Hathaway."

The man shook his head and then smiled. "It is quite obvious that there is little chance of angels being here, Miss Lewis, so the fools must rush in."

As Hathaway paddled toward the float Doris turned to Marcia, perplexity a small frown upon her face. "What gives, doll? How does the character know Valenti?"

"Let's let Valenti worry about that."

Mr. Hathaway seemed to trot beside them as they went back to the house, his alert eyes scanning the location. In the kitchen Booker took one astonished look and thrust an arm across the doorway leading to the living room.

"Who's this?"

"It's all right. He wants to see Valenti." Marcia was almost amused.

"The boss don't want to see no one. You know that."

"He may want to see him. Take your arm down." Marcia pushed it away and Booker, unable to keep up with the situation, stood aside to let them pass. Mr. Hathaway smiled encouragingly at him.

Michael was still at the window, absorbed in his thoughts. Valenti, on the couch, half raised himself and then stared unbelievingly at Hathaway.

"Who's this? Where did he come from?" The words were harsh and edged.

"He's a cop." Marcia seemed to be enjoying herself. "We came to Florida together."

The little man actually flushed. "Now, Miss Lewis," he chided. "That is a very spicy way of putting it, very spicy indeed. And," he grew serious, "you are in error. I assure you I'm not, as you say, a cop."

"Then what were you doing at the police station in Palm Beach?"

"My! Miss Lewis. You are a fount of information." He spoke admiringly. "May I sit down?" He settled himself primly in the chair and neatly crossed his ankles, making a steeple of his fingers and gazing reproachfully over them at Valenti. "You have caused me a great deal of annoyance, Mr. Valenti."

"What the hell goes on here?" Valenti swung his legs from the couch and sat up. "You making some sort of a joke or something. You nuts, maybe?"

"Oh, I assure you I'm in complete possession of all my faculties and this is no joke unless, of course, you view a return to prison as something humorous."

"Look, you." Valenti was tightly furious. "Give out with what you came here to say and then blow. Cop or no cop you got no business here."

"Oh!" Mr. Hathaway was gently admonishing. "You are quite wrong. I do have business here. I thought perhaps we might reach an understanding, since there are complications in this situation of which you are not aware. But I begin to suspect you are an unreasonable man. Under the circumstances I will only say that the moment you put your hands on the money you seek I shall see that you go back to prison. It is something you should think about, Mr. Valenti." He regarded Marcia unhappily. "You, also, Miss Lewis or Mrs. Blake."

"Michael." Valenti's command was whispered.

As Spain started toward the seated figure no one could really believe what he saw but, somehow, without seeming to move, Mr. Hathaway had a revolver in his hand and at the sight of it Spain stopped as though he had been jerked backward by an invisible wire.

"Please don't allow my appearance to deceive you. I dislike being manhandled and so, if you take another step, Mr. Spain, I shall shoot you without any compunction."

To Doris, who was closer and watching, it seemed like a slow-motion sequence from a motion picture. Marcia's arm traveled almost lazily, moving in a leisurely arc as though she were stroking with a tennis racquet. The slender hand, sweeping across the table, closed about the base of a heavy oil lamp and continued on until it crashed against the side of Mr. Hathaway's head.

The man uttered no sound. He bent forward as though he had suddenly grown sleepy. The revolver dropped from his fingers and he teetered on the chair's edge, rocking back and forth for an interminable second before he pitched face down to the floor. Calmly Marcia replaced the lamp upon the table. Doris's sharp intake of breath was the only sound.

Valenti sat looking at the unconscious form and then turned to Marcia with a wolfish grin. "That's a good girl. For the first time I begin to like you. That was real good."

Marcia's lip curled. "Don't thank me. If I didn't need you he could have blown your guts out for all I care. I still think maybe he's a cop, and if he is we're in trouble."

"Is he dead, boss?" Booker was stunned by the rapidity of what had occurred.

"How the hell do I know? Michael. Take a look."

Spain rested on one knee beside Mr. Hathaway, turning the limp body over. A small, whistling sound escaped from between parted lips. Michael stood up.

"Put him on the couch, Hal."

Booker lifted Mr. Hathaway as though he were a baby, bearing him across the room to a couch and then, remembering what he was carrying, dropped him indifferently on the cushions.

Quickly and expertly Michael went through Mr. Hathaway's pockets. He flipped the cards in a wallet and paused over one before tossing it to Valenti.

"Insurance. An investigator. They don't ever give up, do they?"

Valenti's jaw and lower lip were thrust out, giving him the appearance of an aging baboon. He didn't bother to open the wallet, but sat tapping it meditatively against his palm.

"It could be trouble, Michael." He pondered and then raised his eyes to stare at Booker.

The big man backed away. It was an involuntary movement. "Now, boss," he whined. "He's such a little guy. I couldn't rough him up. I'll slap him around some to put some sense in his head." He waited unhappily.

Valenti lifted his eyes to Marcia. "How did he get here?"

"Rowboat with an outboard motor. There's a rod and some bait in it."

"So." Valenti was pleased. "I guess he was out fishing and the boat upsets so he's drowned, he's dead and he doesn't do a lot of talking." He swung around to Spain. "You take care of it, Michael. You and Hal when it's dark but not around here. Down the river someplace."

"Hey!" Doris spoke for the first time. "What are you guys talking about?" She looked around a little wildly. The others ignored her.

"Take the gun too." Valenti commanded. "Drop it in the river, deep. He just never came here. We never saw him." His searching eyes swept the floor. "Where's the gun?"

"I have it." Marcia half leaned against the table and the .38 was in the palm of her hand.

"Well, give it to Michael."

"I think I'll keep it." Marcia clicked the safety catch back and forth.

Valenti stood up quickly, his head drawn menacingly into his shoulders. He started toward her.

The report of the revolver cracked with the sharp explosion of a dynamite cap and a slug tore into the wall beyond Valenti's head. The man halted as though he had been struck. Marcia did not move from her indifferent lounging against the table.

"I can shoot a lot better than that." Her steady gaze held Valenti's. "Just in case anybody gets any ideas, I can shoot a hell of a lot better. I'd hate to lose you, Valenti, and all that money. But if I have to I will. Don't forget it."

CHAPTER TEN

A shrimper, outbound through the inlet at dawn, salvaged Norn's boat, floating bottom up in the sluggish tide. Later in the day a group of youngsters picnicking on the beach were sent into a terrified huddle by the sight of a body rolling clumsily in the light surf. One boy, bolder than than the others, waded out to draw it above the high water mark before they went for help.

In Redemption Cay Bill Longworth sat in the constable's office listening gravely to the medical examiner. He made small, indecipherable scratches on a pad and then impatiently tossed away the pencil, his lips compressed, his eyes angry.

"So," the doctor concluded, "we'll perform an autopsy, but it's a thousand to one you won't find any water in the lungs. A man doesn't breathe much after his neck is broken."

Longworth studied some photographs. "This bruise on the head?" He lifted his eyes.

The medical examiner lit a cigarette. "I don't think so. It knocked him out, maybe. There were marks on his wrists and legs as though he had been tied up. So it looks like whoever had him kept him alive for a while. I don't understand why. His neck was broken and that's pretty hard to do just falling out of a rowboat. I'll mark it in my book as murder. You can take it from there."

Within Longworth now there burned a deep and consuming fury, bringing with it a sensation of nausea. He was always affected this way by criminal violence and wondered, a little helplessly, if he would ever learn to do his job coldly, dispassionately, as an officer of the law should. He wore himself to the thin edge of uncontrolled wrath over each case. It was not society against the lawbreaker but Longworth versus X. He wanted desperately to be objective and always failed.

He sorted again through the effects which had been taken from the body. Some loose bills, a fountain pen, a bunch of keys and the wallet. In Mr. Hathaway's room at the hotel he had made a surprising discovery; a half-filled box of 38-caliber, steel-jacketed cartridges. But there had been no gun and no gun found on the body. It could, of course, have fallen from his pocket when he went overboard. A real nice little man, he mused. But, and this he knew, it wouldn't have made any difference to him if the insurance investigator had been the world's greatest bastard. Murder had been done. Murder. He knew why and by whom but he couldn't prove it. He knew the motive, yes, but nothing more.

"All right, Doc." He stood up. "I'll take your word for it, but let me have an official report as soon as you can."

Outside, drawn by the news of the tragedy and the arrival of county officers, the curious stood in whispering groups. They talked among themselves but their attention was on the small frame building serving as city hall and jail. As Longworth came out a murmur rippled through the crowd. He pushed his way through and halted at the sight of Jeff who stood apart, waiting beside the car.

"All right." Longworth spoke without warmth, friendliness or encouragement. "This is off your beat but I suppose you want to know. Come along and I'll fill you in just in case it spreads out beyond local news." He extended the invitation as something unavoidable. "I'm going to be up to my ass in reporters as soon as someone picks this up at headquarters."

Jeff was a little surprised. "I thought he drowned, that it was an accident."

They were in the car and Longworth pulled out from the curb. "I'll go along with Doc. You have to stretch it some to break your neck falling out of a rowboat." His moody eyes were fixed on a distant point and when he spoke again it was to himself and in anger. "Why the hell would he tackle them alone? It would be like walking through a snake pit barefooted. What would make him go there by himself?"

Jeff was mystified. From the words passed along Main Street he had heard only that a tourist, a Mr. Hathaway, had been drowned, the body washed up on the beach and one of Norn's boats picked up.

"Give it to me from the beginning." Jeff asked. "Where did he go?"

"Valenti has rented a house up Blackfish Creek. I'll lay next year's salary against a burnt match that Hathaway went there. But why? God damn it to hell." His hand smacked viciously at the steering wheel. "Was he trying to make a deal? Did he go bad and offer to back out for a cut? What did he think he had to dicker with? It doesn't make any sense."

"You think Valenti killed him?"

"You're smarter than that, Martin." Longworth was impatient. "Hathaway was on Valenti's back."

Jeff shook his head. "You must have left out a couple of things," he said. "You're not getting through to me."

Longworth smiled unexpectedly. "Well, maybe I did at that." He stopped the car in front of Norn's. "You'll have to walk back. Go on home and figure out what it is that both Valenti and Hathaway were looking for. I'm going to take a boat ride."

Along a stretch of beach Doris walked with fear as her companion. She was way out of her league now and knew it. Killing was something you read about in the newspapers, saw on the screen of a movie or looked at on television. It didn't sit beside you in a room; staring out of the dead fish eyes of a man like Mike Spain, display itself in the clumsy movements of a Hal Booker or the flinty hardness of people like Valenti or Marcia Lewis. I was getting along fine, she told herself. A dumb muff on call, a quick trick kid who took half a bill for a couple of hour's work. How in hell did I get mixed up in this? That doll Marcia was giving her the creeps now. The way she had swung that lamp. The business with a gun and Valenti stopping as though he'd seen the ghost of his mother. Here I am sitting right in the middle of it, knowing something I don't want to know and sooner or later one of them back there is going to realize it and I'm going to be in the way.

She had left them at the house, sitting there, not talking, just quiet, watchful and suspicious with an unbearable tension building up like a thunderhead. Even Booker had been subdued. He washed the breakfast dishes at the sink, shaking his head at her almost timid offer to help.

She had seen nothing, heard nothing, but she knew what had happened. Why it had happened, and why they were afraid of an insurance investigator, particularly a harmless little fellow like that one, she didn't know. Jesus, she said to herself. I wish someone would tell me something. Then she bit on her tongue. I didn't mean it. I don't want to know anything. Panic was an oyster in her throat and she couldn't swallow. Last night, from behind the closed door of her room, to which Valenti had ordered her, she had heard Booker's heavy tread as he went out the back. Seconds later the screen door had slammed a second time. It was too dark to see much but she had glimpsed the shadowy figure of Booker and then Spain going down toward the dock. Minutes later there had been the chattering hum of an outboard motor and after that nothing for a long time. Then the boat returned and she knew Booker and Spain had come back.

For a long time she had sat in the dark room and then, unable to bear the loneliness, had gone out defiantly. Marcia was curled up in a corner of the couch doing her nails. Spain was reading and Valenti was fiddling with the knobs on a portable radio. Booker, an odd and baffling expression of bewilderment on his face, lumbered uneasily about like a newly caged animal. Finally he stopped and poured a large drink of whiskey. She had never seen him take a drink before. He didn't swallow this one. Valenti had turned from the radio and slapped it from his hand.

"You keep away from that. Do you hear?" The old man had been edgy, then he seemed to relent and placed a hand affectionately on Hal's shoulder. "You've got to keep in training, remember?"

"Yeah. Yeah," Booker mumbled. "Yeah, sure, boss."

"That's a good boy." Valenti was smilingly paternal. "Maybe you need a girl, huh, boy?" There was a false note of humor in the question. "A big guy like you. Take Doris. She'll fix you up."

Before she could protest Booker had shaken his head and padded toward the front door. "I'm gonna take a walk." The rickety screen rattled behind him.

Valenti had shrugged. "These big slobs. They're all alike, soft as chicken fat. Give me the little, mean, skinny ones. Maybe"—he glanced at Spain who didn't lift his head—"maybe you can't always trust them but they don't turn to chicken fat. That's why I've always liked you, Michael."

Doris had glanced at Marcia. A faint smile played about her lips as she flicked an emery board at her nails. Valenti sat down abruptly as though his monologue had exhausted him.

Retracing her steps on the beach now, Doris avoided the house, crossing the dunes to walk along the river side until she came to the dock. I want out of this, she kept telling herself, and stood, looking down at the boat Spain had hired, wondering if she could run it. Hell, she thought, I couldn't run water from a tap. Just the same I want out. I don't know what's going on and I don't want anyone to tell me. This is for the real hard ones. I'm just a stupid quiff and I like it that way.

She was still on the dock as Longworth came up the creek, and when he was alongside Doris, for the first time in her life, was glad to see a cop. He merely glanced at her, nodded and allowed the boat to coast to the float. She followed him above on the pier, looking down anxiously, hopefully and waited as he swung himself up to stand beside her.

"Valenti in?" There was no recognition in his eyes and the question was crisply official.

"Up at the house. They're all there." She wanted to say more, to spill it all out in a torrent of words, but fear held her. Beneath his steady gaze she felt as awkward as a tongue-tied adolescent.

There was a sardonic amusement in Longworth's smile but no warmth. "You're softening up a little, aren't you, Doris, where cops are concerned."

Some of her brashness returned. Just having him around made her feel better. "It's the same old pot," she said with a grin. "Only it doesn't get used so much any more. They just have it around to keep flowers in and dress up the place."

He gazed up at the house and then started away towards the sloping path.

"You want me too?" She called uncertainly, hoping he would say yes. Anything was better than being alone.

"I'll get around to you, Doris. I'll get around to everyone."

At the house he didn't bother to knock, pushing open the screen door and allowing it to flap to noisily behind him. In the living room, almost as though they had been expecting him, Valenti, Spain, and Marcia waited for him to speak. Booker, in a chair by the window, started to rise and then sank back; he closed and opened his big hands slowly, staring at them as though the movement fascinated him.

"It's you again, Sheriff." Valenti was undisturbed.

"I thought I'd drop in for a little talk." He roamed about the room, lean and hard; indifferent to them, whistling quietly to himself. "Who killed Hathaway?"

"Who is Hathaway, Sheriff?" Valenti put his feet on the couch and balled a pillow behind his head.

"Uh-uh! We're not going to play that way." He lit a cigarette and dropped the match carelessly on the floor. "We're going to play it my way this time because, you see, someone is going to hang for Hathaway's murder."

"I repeat. Who is Hathaway?" Valenti seemed tired and frail but his eyes were as inky as the discharge of a squid when it tries to escape by clouding the water.

Longworth, almost casually, walked to the couch, snatched Valenti upright by the shoulders and slapped him hard across the face. Neither Booker nor Spain moved. Marcia watched intently as the deputy released Valenti and threw him back upon the couch.

"You'll regret that." Valenti's words were barely audible. "No one hits me and gets away with it."

"I did." Longworth stood waiting and then continued. "Hathaway's body washed ashore this morning. His neck was broken, so it wasn't an accident."

Valenti was surprised, so surprised by the statement that he couldn't control the flick of his eyes as they darted to where Booker sat. Longworth turned slowly and stared at the big man who tried to meet his gaze and failed.

"You could have done it," the deputy mused, "although I figured it was more in Spain's line."

Booker shifted restlessly. "What you talkin' about, huh?" There was a halfhearted defiance in the question. "Why you lookin' at me? I don't know nobody with a name like you said."

Longworth ignored him, directing his words to Valenti. "Prison must have dumbed you up some, Valenti. It could have been an accident. A tourist out fishing, caught in the inlet's current. The coat capsizes and he drowns. Only you had to be sure and so he was killed first. That was real stupid. I think Hathaway came here. Why, I don't know. But you had to get rid of him."

"Is that what you would tell a grand jury, Sheriff?" Marcia's question was derisive. "You think such and such happened. Doesn't a jury usually want more than that?"

"I'll get around to you, Mrs. Blake. Don't be impatient."

"Why don't you stop playing Charley Chan?" Her words crackled scornfully. "You come in here and ask who killed this Hathaway. You think it's a nursery rhyme. 'I, said the sparrow, with my little bow and arrow.'" She laughed openly at him.

Longworth held himself behind a forced casualness. "No, Mrs. Blake. But I'll tell you something." He was amiably confiding. "If we pull at this thing long enough something will snap. That," he added pleasantly, "is right out of the deputy sheriff's manual for home study."

He walked about the room, trying to find some small release from the anger within him by movement. Near the far wall he halted and after a moment took a long-bladed penknife from his pocket. With the point he dug at the wall until a slug dropped into his hand. He examined it carefully and then confronted them again.

"Hathaway was carrying a gun of this caliber. You wouldn't happen to have seen it, would you?" He bounced the pellet in his palm and then put it into his pocket.

"We have target practice every morning." Marcia was tolerant. "Now why don't you go away and give someone a ticket for overtime parking?"

He nodded. "I may just do that, Mrs. Blake, but I'll be back."

He left them and with the closing of the door behind him Valenti began to curse. The filth drooled from his mouth as a flooding sewer and the words were quiet and deadly in their monotone.

He seemed to glide from the couch in a reptilian movement to stand before Booker, who shifted and desperately tried to avoid the accusing eyes. Then Valenti, using the back of his hand, began to hit the big man across the face, the blows falling with the steady beat of a metronome. Booker shuddered and his head rocked back and forth but he made no effort to resist or defend himself from the beating. A ring on Valenti's finger cut at Booker's face and nose and the blood, welling quickly, began to run in small rivulets. He stared piteously, groveling as a beaten dog and his mouth twitched convulsively but he made no outcry.

"You punchy slob." Valenti was breathing heavily from the exertion. "You worm-headed idiot. I might have known you would louse it up."

"It was an accident, boss." The man shuddered as Valenti's hand dropped with a leaden weariness at his side. "He began to put up an argument, twistin' an' tryin' to get away. I didn't figure to do nothin' to him but what you said. He ducked an' I snatched him under the chin, like this." He curved a beefy arm to demonstrate. "How was I to know, boss? It snapped. Just like a chicken bone it broke. Like a little chicken bone you could break with your fingers."

Valenti was trembling. He stood before Booker, shaking uncontrollably, holding a blood-splashed hand before him and then wiping it with the clean one until both were smeared and ugly.

"It should have looked like an accident." Valenti's voice was guttural. "It had to look like an accident but you got to put the arm on heavy an' break his neck first." He spun about to face Spain, who had watched the exhibition of brutality with a mildly interested expression. "You Michael, the smart one, the one I always figured I could trust in a tight spot. Where were you? Where were your brains? A little fellow like that to take care of. Five minutes and it's over. You take him down to the river, hold his head under the water and then you dump him away from here. No. Oh! No. Not the easy, right way. We gotta lean on him. We gotta play strong-arm stuff. We gotta put the muscle on an' leave like it was a callin' card for every cop in the county." Forgotten was the carefully articulated speech which he had cultivated as a façade of gentility. The words were slurred.

"It was an accident, Edward." Spain was not disturbed but he watched Valenti carefully.

"Accident!" Valenti shrieked the word and for a moment seemed on the point of venting his fury upon Spain. Instead, he whirled to strike Booker again as a man might relieve himself of anger by kicking a handy and inoffensive animal.

"Don't hit me no more, boss." Booker swayed back and forth in the torment of humiliation and pain. He blubbered as the tears coursed down his quivering cheeks, mingling with the blood in a scarlet wash. "Please," he was begging, "don't hit me no more that way like I was nothin'. Punch me if you gotta but don't slap me no more. A punch, like I was a man, I can take but I just can't stand no more slappin', boss." His voice rose to the shrill treble of a hysterical woman.

"I oughtta kill you." Valenti was sapped of all strength, his hands shook. "I oughtta open you with a knife an' tear your guts out with my fingers."

"Leave him alone." Marcia's words cracked. "How is this going to help? If you want to beat him take him outside where I don't have to watch."

"Shut up, you. When I need the advice of a cheap—" Valenti's face was purple.

The word he used drew the color from Marcia's cheeks and then her mouth twisted disdainfully. "Just a common hood when it gets tight, aren't you? A gutter rat from Delancey Street dressed up in a monkey suit. When it doesn't go by the book you're lost." She laughed harshly at him.

Valenti dropped limply into a chair. There was no strength left in him. His mouth opened and closed soundlessly.

"It isn't good, Edward." Spain spoke quietly, reassuringly. "It isn't good but it isn't too bad. Sure," he nodded, "the law gets nosy but where does it go from there? Who's going to prove anything? We never saw this fellow. I don't like it, but it's done and we sit on it."

"It's going all wrong, Michael." Valenti adopted a tone of bewildered complaint. "I got a feelin', superstitious-like, that it's sour already an' begins to stink. I got a feelin' to draw back but I can't."

"You don't pull out now, Valenti." Marcia eyed him contemptuously. "Remember that. No one pulls out until we get what we came for."

They paid no attention to Booker as he moved furtively out of his chair and padded heavily across the floor and into the kitchen.

"Don't give me no orders," Valenti muttered, but there was no conviction in his words. "I don't take anything from you."

"Somebody better give you orders." Marcia laughed shortly. "You're coming apart at the seams."

With a deliberate casualness Longworth dropped from the dock to the float, ignoring Doris as she stood almost hopefully, watching his every movement, wanting to speak but unable to find the words. As he untied the boat the deputy glanced up. He was aware of the uneasy apprehension in her eyes.

"Do you want to tell me anything, Doris?" The question was softly voiced, encouraging and friendly.

"Like what?" Speech was difficult, made doubly so by the knowledge that this was her chance and that if she didn't take it there probably wouldn't be another. "What should I want to tell you?"

Longworth settled himself on the narrow, board seat before the motor. "About a man by the name of Hathaway who came here yesterday. What happened to him."

"I didn't see anyone." Fear held her and she was unable to break its grip. Sure, she could open her mouth, tell this cop about the little fellow. The cop might even take her into town with him if she spilled her guts and she'd be away from this. What happened then? There would be no place to hide from Mike Spain or Valenti. No matter where she went, no matter how fast she ran they'd reach out to a thousand connections in as many cities and towns to put the finger on her. "I don't know what you're talking about." She made an attempt at defiance, and failed.

He nodded pleasantly and tapped at the carburetor float. "You're in trouble, Doris. You know that, don't you?" There was no threat in the statements. He made them almost sympathetically. "Accessory after the fact, maybe even before. Withholding information. You'd be surprised at the number of laws they can dig up." He wound the starting cord about the wheel, taking his time and not looking at her.

"Take me with you." She blurted out the words, unable to hold them back.

"Sure, Doris. I'll take you but not just for a boat ride. You'll have to talk. If you do there isn't anything to be afraid of."

"You don't know what you're saying." Involuntarily her head turned and she darted a glance at the house. "Anyhow, I don't know what you want to know. I didn't see anybody here yesterday. You're bowling down the wrong alley."

"Then why do you want to get away?" He was pleasantly interested.

"Because I'm getting trap-happy here." She all but shouted the reply. "There's nothing to do all day and a damn sight less at night. This is for the Swiss Family Robinson but not for a girl like me who likes a kick now and then. Do you figure I'm finding it on top of these God-damned sandhills?" The words raced each other, spurred by desperation and fear. "I just thought maybe you'd take me into town with you and we could have a few drinks and a couple of laughs. That's all. Why do you have to make it a major operation, a big conspiracy?"

Longworth stood up, his hand closing on the dock's planking, holding the boat and halting its drift. His eyes studied Spain's similar craft and then he looked at Doris reflectively.

"Just in case you change your mind."

"I don't know what you're talking about," she interrupted hastily.

"Well. Just in case you do figure out what I'm talking about and want to tell me. Do you know how to run one of these things?"

"No-o-o." Her reply was uncertain. "Why should I?"

"Well. You might need to know." He talked rapidly, pointing to the motor as he explained. "First you turn this valve and set the throttle, this, about here." He looked at the house again. "You wind the cord around this and then pull." He jerked the rope to demonstrate. "That should start it, but you may have to try a couple of times. This." His hand went to the tiller. "This is what you steer with. The motor on that other boat is the same as this one. You go straight down the creek, following those markers; they are the pointed boards on the posts. If you follow them you can't get lost. They'll take you right into the Cay. Understand?"

"Yes. I think so." She was half squatting, her weight resting on one leg, her body inclined forward as she peered at the motor. The light blouse fell away from her tanned shoulders and half down over unencumbered breasts. "But what would I want to know all of that for?" She was still rebellious, or pretending to be, fright and a wild eagerness to get away balancing each other. "Where would I be going?"

"Oh!" He didn't press her. "You just might want to talk with someone; me, for instance. If you do and want to get away before it gets too late you knew how. Take that boat and do just as I told you. You can reach me through the sheriff's office. The name's Longworth. Bill Longworth. You don't have to be afraid. I'll take care of you."

She saw the flick of his eyes as they strayed to where the open blouse revealed her. She tugged at the shoulder with two fingers, indolently pulling it back into place, but her grin was ribald and filled with delighted malice that even her gnawing terror could not subdue.

"Yeah." She slurred the word provocatively and her glance traveled over him with a new interest. "I guess you would take care of me at that. Keep your mind on your business, Sheriff, whatever it is."

Her words forced the faintest of smiles from him. "I'm trying to, Doris. But you make it difficult in that pose. I'll go that far. You make it damn difficult You're sure you don't want to change your mind?"

She wanted to scream yes, to drop from the dock and into the boat, putting the miles between her and Valenti and what had happened. But there were no miles long enough. This she knew. She shook her head, unable to speak, and after a moment's hesitation he shoved the boat away from the dock, started the motor and swung in a wide half-circle to head down the creek.

Doris watched him until the small craft was out of sight, wishing, now that it was impossible, that she had gone with him, but knowing she was a dead pigeon from the moment Valenti would learn of her action. You'll just sweat this one out kid, she told herself desperately; maybe, after it's over, you can hang your clothes on that hickory limb and never go near the water. Just dumb up good from here on in and be like those monkeys. See nothing. Hear nothing. Say nothing. Maybe you can stay alive.

Reluctantly she turned and began to walk toward the house, halting abruptly at the spectacle of Booker as he shuffled dazedly down the path.

"Good God! What happened to you?" She was appalled at his appearance and the broken, stumbling gait.

The big man was crying. He wept unashamedly, blubbering noisily through mucus and tears. His face had begun to puff in a lopsided formation and the blood was drying, making of his features a tortured and grotesque mask. He stood before her licking at his swollen lips.

"Who's been working on you, ape?" She took his arm, almost feeling sorry for him. "Did Mike Spain do this? Why?" She really didn't want to know. This was what happened when you stepped out of line. What could have happened to her if she had gone with that sheriff, thinking it was a quick and easy way out.

"The boss got mad, he got real mad." Booker's sluggish mind groped toward a satisfactory answer. "Honest, Dorrie, I didn't figure it would happen that way. He was such a little guy. I hardly touched him but it cracked like a match stick. The boss got real sore at me." He seemed dazed but not resentful over what had happened. There was no anger in him but a bewildered sense of injury to his feelings. "Honest, Dorrie. It was like I said. An accident."

"Don't tell me anything. Do you hear, Booker? I don't want to hear anything. I don't want to know anything. Understand?"

"Sure, Dorrie." He was uncomprehending. "Sure. Whatever you say."

She hesitated briefly and then dropped from the dock to the float. "Come here." She called to him. When he lowered himself and stood beside her she bent and dipped a handkerchief into the water. "Jesus. What a mess." She was awed by the close examination of the lacerated flesh. With surprising gentleness she washed his face, softening the dried blood, and at the touch of the salt water he winced.

"That hurts, Dorrie. That hurts real bad," he protested but did not pull away, seeming to take a childlike pride in his ability to bear the discomfort and anxious for a word of approval.

"You're a lug, Hal. Just a big, dumb lug." She rinsed the handkerchief out and applied fresh water.

"You never called me Hal before. Do you know that, Dorrie? It was always Ape, like you were kidding." He smiled, happy with this new intimacy.

"Sure. I'm always kidding. A girl for the laughs." She replied absently, her mind ranging to a movie she had seen a long time ago about a man who had created a monster to do his bidding. He just pushed a button and the thing did what it was told. Booker might be the monster and a way out of this. The idea startled her.

"Yeah." She repeated, "Always kidding. Little Doris, a peck of fun for young and old."

"Why are you bein' so nice to me now, Dorrie?" He was puzzled. "Maybe you really like me a little? I always liked you."

"Sure. Everybody likes me. Doris with the heart of gold." She stepped back to study his face. "You look better. What the hell did Valenti use, a pair of scissors?"

"I never seen him so mad before, Dorrie. He was like a wild man, the way he screamed. I guess he's got a lot on his mind we don't know about." He was in a quandary, divided now between a stubborn loyalty to Valenti and a desire to please her.

She dug into her blouse pocket for a cigarette, understanding how cautiously she must walk. "You don't have to take something like this from anyone, Hal." She darted a quick glance at the house, as though her words might be heard even at this distance. "Why!" She touched his arm admiringly. "I'll bet you could handle Valenti and Mike Spain with one hand at the same time."

"Sure. Sure I could. They don't keep in trainin', see? I'm in shape all the time. But," his face clouded doubtfully, "I wouldn't never lay a hand on the boss no matter what he did. He's been real good to me."

"I could be good to you, Hal." She breathed the words, her eyes holding his. Her hand slid caressingly over his forearm and glided through an opening in the shirt and across his bare chest. She could feel the rippling movement of his skin. "Did you ever think about that? Say, maybe, we just had a chance and were alone together?" Her leg brushed his and remained to rest there with an insinuating pressure. Her voice was throaty and low.

"Aw! You're kiddin', Dorrie." He was incredulous, wanting to believe but ready to pretend he knew it was a joke all the time if she laughed. "Like you said." His throat moved convulsively. "Anything for a gag?" His eyes were hungry with the question.

She shook her head. "I wouldn't kid you about that. Give me your hand. I'll show you I mean it." When he shifted uneasily on his feet she smiled with a sad, helpless expression and reached to take his fingers, drawing herself closer to him and then softly placing his hand on her breast, pressing against it with a sharp gasp of pain at the contact. Her eyes widened. "You're so big, Hal. So big and strong. Do you know how that makes a girl feel?"

He wet his lips and his thick fingers closed on her breast. "The boss would kill us if he saw this. You don't know what he's like."

"I wouldn't be afraid if you were with me." She seemed to cling to him. "What do I want with an old man like that? We could go away together. We could slip out tonight and take that boat." She fed it to him warily. "How would you like that, just the two of us?"

"You don't know what you're sayin', Dorrie." His hand was punishing her breast but she did not draw away. "He'd come after us or send somebody. He wouldn't like it if I took his girl."

"I'm just your girl, Hal. If you want me you would have to take care of him first; maybe Mike Spain, too. A lot of things could happen, like the house catching on fire and they couldn't get out." She waited anxiously, felt him stiffen with resentment.

"Not the boss." He withdrew his hand and pulled away from her. His eyes were small, filled with suspicion. "You ain't askin' me to do anythin' to the boss? I wouldn't like to hear you say that, Dorrie." There was a stubborn, idiotic resentment behind the words.

"Then you are a lug after all." She carelessly snapped the cigarette away. "He cuts your face to hamburger and," she mimicked him, "you don't want to do nuttin' about it. Jesus. Am I a sucker. I thought I had a real man at last." She was impatient.

"He was only mad, Dorrie." He tried to placate her. "I did a dumb thing, I guess, an' that made him mad. He didn't mean nothin' by what he did. It was just like I made him mad, that's all." His expression was stricken.

"Then you're just a dumb ape. You don't know what you want." She was tormenting him and knew it.

"No I ain't really." He made a fumbling effort to touch her again but she shook him off. "Gee! Dorrie. You feel good. It's like I never touched a girl before. I never figured you liked me this way."

"I could like you a lot." She was intense. "You're big and strong. That's what a girl wants, but she's got to be proud of her man, too. How do you think it makes me feel when I see Valenti and Spain push you around? Who the hell do they think they are?"

"Yeah?" He was still doubtful. "Who the hell do they think they are?" Just repeating her words seemed to give him confidence. "You maybe got somethin'. Who the hell do they think they are?" His mind worked over this startling idea with ponderous gravity. "But"— his features clouded doubtfully again—"I don't know. The boss."

She knew she had him. He was on the hook. What surprised her was her own attitude. She had set Valenti and Spain up and the knowledge didn't disturb her. It's them or it's me; maybe not here, not right now, but sooner or later they're going to tell each other Doris knows too much. So what happens if she runs off at the mouth? She didn't want to admit the answer to herself. Who would miss another muff? That was the way they would figure it.

"Maybe you'd meet me tonight down on the beach, Dorrie?"

Booker's words broke into her thoughts. "Maybe." She wasn't enthusiastic.

"No." He remembered something and was a child in his disappointment. "No. We couldn't make it tonight. The boss said I had to go into that crappy town with Spain this evening. But we could make it some other time. How about it, Dorrie?" Furtively his fingers reached out to stroke her hair. "You're like a real, soft kitten, Dorrie. Every time I look at you I want to pet you like this an' put my hand on your hair. It's sure pretty hair, Dorrie." He chuckled gleefully, a foolish chatter of excitement. The sound of his voice made her shiver.

Faintly there came to the dock the loose banging of the screen door at the back of the house. Doris glanced up quickly and moved away from Booker with studied casualness. Marcia was coming down the path.

"It's that doll," she whispered, making him a partner in a conspiracy. "Now, you don't say anything. Just be dumb, huh, ape?"

He grinned foolishly. "Yeah! Sure, Dorrie. Whatever you say. We let on like we was just talkin', huh? Anything you say."

CHAPTER ELEVEN

The residents of the Cay tested the unfamiliar word. Murder. It came easily after the first shock of surprise had worn off and they sent it winging from house to house, over back fences, from corner to corner and store to store until it was almost possible to feel the tense excitement as an invisible current in the air.

All day Jeff had avoided Jim Patrick, knowing the photographer would press him, either on his own or through orders from Burrows. After leaving Longworth he had taken his car and driven to the County Hospital hoping he would find Judy there; knowing with an empty feeling that when he did there would be nothing to say, no excuse to give. The floor nurse had been as crisp as the linen she wore. Mr. Carter's condition was satisfactory. The words came by rote. At his daughter's instructions no visitors were permitted. He understood well enough that by visitors Judy meant him. Troubled, unhappy and trapped within a web of indecision he had left the hospital and found a small bar, sitting alone and brooding over a drink he didn't want. Finally, he shoved it aside and went back to the Cay.

There were reporters from Miami and one from West Palm Beach asking questions of Norn, and the constable, and Abernathy at the hotel. They received plenty of answers but they didn't add up. An insurance investigator by the name of Hathaway had been killed; no one really knew why. Bill Longworth did but he brushed off the question. Jeff, on his part, had moved closer to the reason but he hadn't put it into words yet, even to himself.

Because there was no place else to go he parked outside the Fish Shack, knowing he would find Patrick there but no longer caring.

The place was crowded, buzzing with excited talk. Patrick was on a stool at the end of the bar. He lifted his glance at Jeff's entrance and nodded without cordiality, almost impersonally. For a moment Jeff was tempted to keep the bar's length between them and then he said to hell with it. He pushed into the scant inches of space beside the photographer.

"Where the hell have you been all day? I left a couple of notes for you at the hotel. Big excitement in town."

"Local stuff?" Jeff shook his head in reply to Bud's questioning glance.

"I don't know." Patrick was suspicious. "I've got the damnedest feeling you are holding out on me again. I talked with Burrows. He called."

"That would figure." At the moment Jeff didn't give a damn about Grant Burrows, his job or whether he ever saw New York again.

"He's sore as hell." Patrick shoved an ice cube around in his drink with one finger, not looking at Jeff. "He wanted to know what was going on. They had a stick or so from the AP on this Hathaway killing. Burrows doesn't think it's only local either." He regarded Jeff with shrewd thoughtfulness.

"Let Burrows come down and cover it."

"He put Joe Montgomery on the Hathaway business in New York." Patrick still watched him. "The insurance company's home office wouldn't give out with anything. Said Hathaway was on a vacation. Burrows sort of figures this is a hell of a place to come to get your neck broken. He thinks that's real funny."

"Let him laugh then."

"Kid." Patrick was honestly concerned now. "You didn't marry the publisher's daughter, remember that. You could be fired."

"Do you know something?" For the first time Jeff displayed any interest in the conversation. "At the moment I don't give a damn. I almost wish he would fire me. Son of a bitch!" The senseless curse exploded. "I came down here on a vacation. I'm not supposed to be working."

Patrick smiled and crooked a finger in Bud's direction. "Give my friend here a drink even if he says no." When the boy had put out a glass and left them to the bottle Patrick shook his head. "Whores, reporters and cops. They're never off duty. You know that." He took a meditative swallow of his drink. "What became of Cartright? I found out where he and his daughter live and went down there, but no one was around. I got a couple of shots of the boat and the canal. We can dress this one up real good when you get around to a typewriter but I want some pictures of the judge and the girl. Where are they?"

"I don't know." The lie came easily and he swallowed it with the bourbon.

Patrick shrugged. "All right, kid. I'll find out. You know that. I got time and an expense account. That's an almost unbeatable combination."

Jeff didn't want an argument with Patrick. They had been good friends for too long. "Thanks for the drink." He edged back through the standing men and turned for the door. "I'll see you later."

Outside he sat in the car smoking a cigarette. Most of the town seemed to be on the streets. The night had come swiftly and they stood about in the patches of light cast by store windows, talking, looking up with interest at the approach of everyone who came their way, eager for any snatch of gossip or information. He leaned his head against the cushion, staring at the star-filled sky. A southeast wind drifted along Main Street and brought with it the sound of the ocean, the smell of the sea and hot sand. Finally he switched on his lights, turned the ignition and starter key.

He drove the length of Main Street and to the curving shell road that wound about the riverfront. Although he knew Judy would still be at the hospital or in a nearby motel he was irresistibly drawn here. Along this stretch they had walked hand in hand. In the shadow of those bootjack palms they had sat, experiencing the wonder of just being together. He had made love to her there and could still hear her gasp of sweet agony as they reached fulfilment together. And, later, the cigarette they had shared between them and as it passed from mouth to mouth it became an instrument of love.

As he turned from the road into what was little more than a track beaten in the high grass on the edge of the marsh he stiffened behind the wheel and then hit the accelerator, the car leaping like a startled jackrabbit. From the distant houseboat thin cracks of light appeared along the edges of drawn curtains. They had come home.

He skidded to a halt within the cleared patch surrounded by marsh and all but leaped from the car. He had to see her, to erase the memory of what she had said and the way she looked on that last night together. The judge would understand. He knew that, and that through him he might be able to reach Judy. He had to reach her because now, what he did and said, ate or drank, were all meaningless. In this moment he knew he was through as a reporter for the *Globe.* Maybe he was through as a newspaperman. If you couldn't keep a story objective, you were no good to your paper. He wasn't going to write the Cartright story. The damage had been done; it was his foot that had kicked the stone starting the avalanche, but someone else would have to take it from here.

He strode hurriedly along the path and halted at the edge of the gangplank.

"Judy?" His voice echoed.

What happened then caused him to stand transfixed. The light in the cabin snapped out and there was no sound. Then, startling enough to send a chill down his back, the insane laugh of a loon cackled over the flats.

"Judy?" He called again and save for his voice the marsh was wrapped in a heavy blanket of silence.

He went aboard, the gangplank creaking and swaying beneath his weight. At the cabin door he knocked. There was no reply, no betraying sound from within. He was momentarily angry. This was stupid and Judy was an intelligent girl. She must understand she couldn't continue to avoid him. She had heard his voice, recognized it. Otherwise, he reasoned, why should the light have been extinguished?

He waited and with each passing second an uneasy prickling sensation crept at the base of his neck. There was no sound, no movement to provoke it but it was there. For a long time, or so it seemed, he stood with his hand on the knob. Behind the door he could sense an alien, dangerous presence. It was as though a silent and poisonous fog drifted about him with unrecognizable menace. He turned the knob slowly and heard the faint snick of the latch as it was sprung free. With his fingertips he pushed the panel until the door swung open. The cabin was a square of darkness in which nothing moved but something waited.

"Judy?" He whispered the word, not quite understanding why. "Judy? Are you there?" The seconds were interminable. Every instinct told him to be careful and in this moment he was the primitive man, cautious as an animal, actually sniffing for the scent of an enemy. It was sheer atavism; the centuries of civilization had been stripped away. "Judy?" He did not move.

It happened then, although later when he tried to remember, he could recall no warning, no small sound. His head simply exploded with flashing streaks of light and he pitched drunkenly through the cabin's doorway and crashed heavily upon the floor.

When he moved it was with no recollection of what had happened. His head felt as sodden as a huge, wet sponge. He lay there and consciousness trickled back in small dribbles. He attempted to lift his head and it fell back limply, slapping his mouth against rough boards. The blow was painful and its shock accelerated his return to full consciousness. He licked at his mouth and tasted the salt-sweet blood from a cut where his teeth had sliced into a lower lip. After a few more seconds he pulled himself to hands and knees, palms flat against the boards, arms tremblingly rigid to brace his weight. Then slowly, painfully, he drew himself up and settled back on his haunches.

He took a deep breath. Whoever had been in the cabin had gone. He knew he was alone. Fumbling for a tab of matches and striking one he shielded the tiny flame with cupped hands. It was an uncertain light at best but by it he had a second or so to see the disorder of the cabin. The paper stick blackened and curled away. He lit another and this time made his way unsteadily across what had been the cabin's floor, hazardous now with ripped planking and scattered objects. There was a kerosene lamp on the galley's sink.

When he lifted the glass chimney it was still warm. He knew then he hadn't been out very long if the lamp had not cooled. The flame crept about the circular wick and he replaced the chimney. Light flooded the cabin and holding it above his head he stared about, unwilling, almost, to believe what he saw.

The cabin had been torn apart, literally ripped away. A crowbar lay across the splintered floor boards as they had been pried from the two-by-fours supporting them. Holes gaped to the bilge. Cushions and mattresses had been ripped open, their contents tossed about as though someone had worked with a mounting fury of frustration. The galley cabinet doors were ajar, the pans and boxes they had held strewn indifferently in all directions. China lay in sharp and broken fragments. Even the tiny galley oven had been torn apart, its sides forced away from the stove. There was not a single square foot of the cabin that had not been systematically and ruthlessly searched. He experienced an angry sickness, remembering Judy's quiet pride in its order, its sparkling neatness. Then—and the thought caused a cold sweat to break over his body—he wondered what would have happened if she and the judge had been at home. This was no ordinary vandalism, no purposeless destruction of an empty home.

He shook his head and the movement caused it to ache and pound. Carrying the lamp to avoid falling through the torn planking, he made his way outside and then blew out the light. Nothing here had been disturbed. Whoever had searched the cabin had been interrupted before the outside deck lockers and deck planking could be investigated.

He sat in the darkness, elbow on knees, head in hand, and began to experience the first real anger he had ever known. He'd been sore plenty of times, mad enough to fight, but now he wanted to kill, to feel bones and flesh give way beneath his hands and heels. This was a slow, burning wrath that would not consume itself quickly. He had seen no car parked anywhere along the marsh's edge, so they must have come by the river and then up the creek. If so then he had been out for longer than he thought, for there had been no sound of a boat's motor and nothing moved upon the river now unless it was being silently propelled by oars.

He stood up and for a second his head swam, then cleared. He took a deep breath of the cool air and felt better. The judge had no right to jeopardize any life but his own. He could not expose Judy this way. If he had to he'd beat the truth out of the old rummy. He went to the gangplank and crossed to the shore.

Indifferent to the slamming springs and the dangerous swaying of the car he bore down upon the gas pedal, hurtling recklessly through the night while his headlights stabbed out a path in the darkness.

On Main Street he skidded to a stop before the City Hall. An office was lighted at the back of the building. He ran up the few steps, tried the door and found it unlocked. His footsteps echoed as he strode quickly down the dark and silent hall.

Bill Longworth sat at a scarred desk beneath a green-shaded overhead light. There was a soggy container of cold coffee before him and the floor was littered with half-smoked cigarettes. He looked up at the door's opening.

"What happened to your head?" The deputy swung about and regarded his visitor with interest.

Jeff placed a hand tenderly over the swollen knob at his temple and glanced into a small wall mirror. The lump was turning a sunset purple. He kicked out a chair and sat down facing Longworth.

"You'd better put a guard over Cartright at the hospital, and maybe one over Judy, too."

The deputy nodded, displaying no surprise at the suggestion. "There's one sitting outside his door now. I hadn't thought about the girl. Maybe it's a good idea."

Jeff relaxed a little and then grinned sheepishly. "I guess that came from reading too many detective stories. You know, where the wise reporter always makes dummies out of the cops and shows them how to solve everything. I guess I should have known you would have it figured this way. Sorry."

"All right. Tell me, what happened to you?" Longworth shoved a package of cigarettes Jeff's way and waited until he had one lit. "Who worked you over and why?"

Jeff told him. "If I hadn't interrupted them," he concluded, "I think they would have taken that houseboat apart plank by plank. It would be driftwood in the inlet by now."

Longworth took a swallow of the coffee and shuddered. "That's awful stuff." He leaned back in his chair. "You know what they want." It was a statement, not a question.

"Yeah. I guess so." Jeff shook his head wearily. "But I can't figure a man sitting on a million or so dollars for over twenty years and I still don't know how he got it or why he has it."

"I do." Longworth's expression was as flat as his words. He bent to open a bottom drawer, drew out and uncapped a fifth of bourbon. "I've been wondering who I could have a drink with. I didn't want to do it alone. You came along at the right time." He uncoiled himself, went to a washbasin and took a couple of stained jelly glasses from a shelf, filling them with tap water.

They both took a long slug straight from the bottle. Jeff waited until the first hit bottom and he could feel its creeping warmth in his stomach. Then he took a second. Longworth helped himself.

"You've picked a shady character for a father-in-law." He mused. "Maybe, here in the Cay, he adds up as a benign old tosspot, but that isn't quite the way it's put together. I've spent a lot of the county's money today on long-distance calls to New York and Washington. What I found out develops a pretty sharp picture and a lot of interesting theory but none of it is provable yet. I know and you know who tore up the houseboat but I can't prove it. Somewhere there's a million and a quarter dollars, more or less; Cartright knows where it is because he brought it here. That's assuming it is here. If it isn't in the Cay, then the judge knows where it is hidden. Offhand I'd say the knowledge was dynamite. One man has already been killed. Hathaway was a threat and a nuisance and that's why he got it."

Jeff shook his head. What Longworth said had to be true, otherwise this didn't make much sense.

"You don't honestly think Judge Cartright had anything to do with the lift itself, do you?"

The deputy shook his head. "No. He was sucked into it. What I found out today you would have discovered if you were in New York and had time to nose around a little. Edward Valenti made Cartright. He brought him up through the city's politics from a municipal bench to the high court. Cartright was Valenti's man and Valenti handled him as carefully as a good manager might spot a promising young fighter on his way to the champion-ship. This wasn't hard to do. Valenti was a power. His influence reached into every ward in New York. Cartright was ambitious and ambition made him weak, not strong as it does some men. He took the easy way, the sure way."

Longworth paused for a moment, his eyes on the ceiling, hands locked behind his head.

"Something else happened. These two men, set poles apart, became friends. Cartright was grateful. He did what he was told, but if Valenti had a friend it was Cartright. They saw a lot of each other. In his way Valenti copied Cartright; his gracious manner, his poise. He even developed a sinister charm of sorts. Then"— he paused and whistled thoughtfully—"Cartright married Maria Alberni. The Italians are a sentimental people. Having his friend married to a countrywoman seemed to tie Valenti closer. Cartright began turning up in Hot Springs, Miami, Agua Caliente when Valenti and his boys were there. Cartright knew what made the wheels move, saw them put into motion. At the political dinners, the ward clambakes and closed sessions Cartright sat at Valenti's right hand. The syndicate had New York tied into knots in those days. It controlled the dope, the girls, the wire rooms, numbers racket, longshoremen, trucking companies, the fish and produce markets. The judge was on his way to the Governor's chair with Valenti smoothing out the road."

"All of that figures." Jeff interrupted. "But this armored car job? Where does the judge fit in?"

"The armored car holdup didn't go through channels. That was the big trouble. A few of the boys thought they were smarter than Valenti and went off on their own. The syndicate permitted these operations only after it had studied and approved the job. The renegades didn't ask for approval or permission. There was no cut for Valenti. So he had the boys pulled in and laid it on the line. Insubordination only paid off with a bullet in the head and the mob knew it. So they brought in the loot and turned it over to Valenti. He probably told them they would have to wait until the money cooled off. But, and here was the problem, he couldn't bank it. He sure couldn't carry it around in his pocket. The only person he believed he could really trust was Cartright, and Cartright doublecrossed him. The boys went to jail, Valenti with them, and this must have been one hell of a big surprise. The judge had a million and some dollars and Valenti was behind the walls for twenty years."

Jeff was still mystified. "Why should Cartright have crossed Valenti? He had everything to lose."

Longworth, leaning back in his chair, balanced precariously for a moment and then leaned forward. The front legs hit the floor with a thump. He pushed the bottle toward Jeff.

"From here on in," he spoke slowly, "I think, maybe, you're going to need a drink."

Puzzled, Jeff studied the deputy and then shook his head.

"All right." Longworth almost sighed. "You're not going to like it. Maybe you won't even believe it. Cartright sent Valenti to jail for the maximum sentence because he found out Valenti had taken his wife." He lifted a hand to ward off Jeff's protest. "Wait a minute." He cautioned. "I'm not just a deputy sheriff in Florida putting together something that happened a long time ago. This came from the top. Maria Alberni Cartright was young, intent upon a career. She wasn't satisfied to be the wife of Judge Amos Cartright. Valenti spelled a lot of power. Maybe she even fell in love with him; who the hell can answer that? Don't ever believe that your best friend won't lay your wife. Homicide records prove he'll be the first to do it. Aside from what she may or may not have felt for Valenti, Maria Alberni knew he could help her career. Hell! If he wanted to he could buy the Metropolitan Opera Company for her. So there they were. The old, old triangle. A hot, ambitious girl and Valenti, always on the prowl for something new."

Longworth poured himself a drink this time and sipped it slowly, staring again at the ceiling.

"All right. Get on with it." Jeff's words were harsh. He knew now what the answer had to be. "Or should I finish it for you?"

"It might be better if you did." Longworth slid the glass the table's length. "Maria Alberni Cartright went to Reno and got a divorce. It was done quietly and Valenti saw to it that the news never went any farther than the usual legal notice in the local papers. Maria may have thought Valenti would marry her. He didn't. Why the hell should he? He could have all the girls he wanted. Maria was pregnant."

"Judy." Jeff whispered the name.

Longworth nodded. "She's Valenti's daughter. Pride, or whatever you want to call it, kept Maria silent when she found out Valenti's intentions were strictly dishonorable. She had her child in a small town in the Catskills, giving as its father's name the name of her own father, Rico Alberni. That is how the birth certificate reads. She told Cartright, though. He took care of her and the child after it was born. Three or four years later Maria died of cancer. Cartright took the child. Why he did this no one but the judge could tell you. Maybe he was still in love with Maria. Men have done stranger things. The FBI now figures that when the judge disappeared he hid out in this mountain community before he made the move down here."

Stunned, but knowing what Longworth had said was true, Jeff reached for the bottle and then put it down again.

"It shook me up a little, too." Longworth was sympathetic. "But I don't see why it has to go any farther than this room. If for all these years Cartright has kept it from her, then it's something between them. All I want to do is prevent another murder—the judge's." He rose and strode impatiently up and down the room. "I wonder if they found anything on that houseboat? Valenti wouldn't get rid of the judge until he found what he was looking for."

"I don't know," Jeff replied mechanically. He was thinking about Judy, knowing now that he had to handle the Judge Cartright story to keep Burrows from sending down another man, a man who would learn what Longworth had just told him and write it for everyone to read. That way he could at least keep Judy's identity out of the story. "If they did, the judge is a sitting duck."

"Maybe not. It could be that all Valenti wants is the money. You can lose your thirst for revenge after that many years in prison. Anyhow, the money isn't my job. The murder of Hathaway is."

"Can't you take them all in on suspicion?"

"I can take them in but I can't hold them." He shook his head. "This is the kind of a job that keeps you twitching at night. I know who did it but I haven't any proof. I've got an idea someone is going to break. She's scared now. When she decides it's better to be scared of Valenti than of me, she'll give. Well." He picked up his hat. "I need some sleep."

Jeff stood up. "I'm going to find Judy." He hesitated. "But first I want to see Jim Patrick, and then—well, I'd like to talk with the judge. Can you fix it for me at the hospital?"

Longworth examined his hat as though he were seeing it for the first time. Then, he nodded and reached for the telephone, calling the hospital and finally getting the head nurse.

"Cora? Bill Longworth. Fine. Yourself? Good. A friend of mine"— he squinted at Jeff half-humorously—"a reporter, wants to see one of your patients. Carter. I have a man outside his door. Yes. That's the one. Let him in as a favor, will you? The name's Jeff Martin. Tell Clifton at the door I said it was all right. Thanks." He dropped the receiver in its cradle and put on his hat. "I still need that sleep."

CHAPTER TWELVE

Jim Patrick, *half* turned on his stool, facing the door of the Fish Shack's bar, saw Jeff as he entered and nodded reservedly. Patrick was a conscientious newspaperman and he disapproved of the way a big story was being handled. There were half a dozen other customers ranged on either side of him. Two were reporters from Miami sheets and they had been talking shop.

"See you for a minute, Jim?" Jeff indicated one of the small booths.

Patrick picked up his half-filled glass and followed. He sat down, lit a cigarette and regarded Jeff unhappily.

"You're getting too cagey for me, Scoop." He shook his head sadly. "What's the pitch now?"

"No pitch. We're going in with it. Get the pictures off to Burrows. I'll put an overnight on the wire to the desk and they can have everything by the time the lobster trick comes on. It will be in galleys by the time Burrows sits down."

Patrick swallowed the remainder of his drink. "It's about time. The way you have been sitting on it I thought we were hatching an ostrich egg. Anyhow, the pictures have already gone. I printed them myself in a local photographer's shop. Where do you expect to find a Western Union open here at this time of night?"

"I'll phone it in to West Palm Beach or Miami."

"Have you written it yet?" Patrick was still suspicious.

"No, but I will."

"Are you leveling with me, kid?"

Jeff flushed with anger, but then the memory of their long association made him grin. "Almost." He tried to make it sound like a joke and succeeded.

Patrick nodded. "I guess that's good enough. Let's have a drink together."

Jeff shook his head and stood up. "I've got some things to do. I'll see you later, or in the morning." He turned and left quickly before Patrick could protest....

At the hospital he introduced himself to the head nurse, who took him to the second floor and down the long and silent corridor to where a man sat. His chair was tilted against the wall and he was relaxed in a precarious balance.

"This is the reporter Bill phoned about."

The deputy nodded disinterestedly. "If it's okay with Longworth it's sure all right with me. Go on in. He's awake. I just looked."

Jeff closed the door behind him and stood peering at the sheet-covered figure. The features were haggard and gaunt under the soft glow of a night light. The eyes were open but they stared without recognition. He stepped forward a few paces.

"Judge Cartright."

The eyes flickered for a second. "Oh! It's you, Mr. Martin."

"Will you talk with me for a few minutes?"

"Do I have a choice?"

"No, sir. At least, I'll talk to you. Maybe you won't answer, but I think you will."

An indistinct smile traced its way across the sagging mouth. "My boy." Something of the old, robust gusto was in the voice's timbre. "I've spent a lifetime talking. I do it better on whiskey. You wouldn't have had the foresight to put a small flask somewhere about your person would you?"

"No." He moved a chair close to the bed and sat down.

The judge sighed. "I didn't think so. Do you know? It is rumored that the St. Bernard dogs no longer carry the traditional casks of brandy about their necks in the Alps. Now it's a first-aid kit with vitamin pills, bandages and concentrated rations. It is a dismal world, and getting no better." He closed his eyes as though the effort of talking had been too much. His face appeared to collapse into folds of grey dough and the paunch beneath the coverlet shrank.

Alarmed, Jeff started to reach for the call bell which would bring a nurse. A weary motion of the judge's hand halted him.

"I'm all right." The words were clear. "What can I do for you?"

"You can save your life."

"This poor, worm-eaten thing? It is a subject which holds little interest for me."

"Then you can think of Judy. I went to your houseboat this evening. It had been torn apart. Valenti, a man named Michael Spain and a big muscle, Booker, have rented a place on the other side of the river. You know what they're after, and they won't leave until they get it."

"Edward was always a man of little imagination. Cunning, shrewd, relentless, mind you, but not inventive. Did he honestly believe I would insulate the walls of a houseboat with a million or more dollars in bills?"

"I was cracked on the head by someone I never saw." Jeff was impatient. "Suppose Judy had been there alone? That's why I say you have to think of her."

"You're in love with my daughter, aren't you?"

"That hasn't a damned thing to do with it. All right. So I'm in love with her. Don't you understand what I'm telling you?" He leaned forward earnestly. "A man by the name of Hathaway, an insurance investigator, was murdered yesterday because he was in Valenti's way. Do you think for a moment you can expect better treatment?"

"But, of course, my boy. I told you before I would be of no value to Edward dead. You see, I know what he wants to know and there is no voice from the tomb."

"Suppose he tries to work on you through Judy?"

For a moment there was no reply. The only sound was a long breath, drawn unsteadily and held.

"That would be the ultimate in tragic jest." The words were whispered with the expelled air.

"The photographs which were taken of you have already gone to New York. I'm putting the story on the wire tonight. Do you know why I'm doing that, Judge Cartright?"

"I suppose each man has his own particular form of infamy, Mr. Martin." The eyes opened again.

"I'm doing it." Jeff spaced his words carefully. "I'm doing it because if I don't my city desk will send another man down. He's a good man, one of the best. He'll dig and pry until he finds out what I have and then every newspaper in the country will print the story that Judy is Edward Valenti's daughter. Is that what you want to happen?" He grabbed the old man's arm and shook him vigorously. "Is it?"

The eyes staring from the bed were bleak as a winter's twilight, terrible in a glaring malignancy. Jeff had never looked upon such impotent fury. Then the mouth, slack and bubbling with spittle a moment ago, tightened and character grew upon the face. An inner power, a final summoning of will, forced a weak and ravaged body into a sitting position.

"Turn on the light, Mr. Martin." There was no uncertainty in the voice now. It commanded and would not be denied. "Let me see the sort of man I am talking with."

Jeff went to a wall switch near the door and flicked it. The spotlessly efficient room was brought into sharp focus by the overhead light. He stood waiting while the figure in the bed studied him. It was a dissection by one who had seen all manner of evil. Finally, the massive head nodded slowly as if its eyes had sought for and found what they needed to know.

"What would you print, Mr. Martin? What will you write when you sit alone in front of a typewriter? I will believe what you tell me now."

Jeff sighed with relief and returned to his chair. "I will write only what you tell me in this room. If you choose not to mention your daughter Judy as other than your daughter, then as far as I know she is Judy Cartright."

"We have to go back many years." Amos Cartright began his story. He repeated substantially what Longworth had told Jeff earlier. It was a sinister pattern, crisscrossed by greed, ambition, power and weakness, love, honesty, lies, hate. When it was finished the old man sagged weakly and dropped upon his pillows, exhausted. Jeff moved his chair back.

"No." The judge whispered. "Not yet. There is something you have to do for me. In the closet there, find my shoes and bring the one for the left foot."

Jeff stared, not believing what he had heard. Then, he went to the closet and returned with the designated shoe.

"There's a spoon in a glass on the table. Take it and pry off the heel."

Jeff worked with the spoon's lip and the heel came off easily. He turned it in his hand and in a hollowed-out section there was a thin, flat square of oiled silk. It was stained from seepage but whatever it contained was intact. He glanced inquiringly at the judge, waiting for instructions.

"I have carried that with me for a long time. Whenever I bought a new pair of shoes I took off one heel, hollowed it out and replaced it with that inside. At the time I thought of it only as a symbol of evil which I would carry with me. Now, though, it serves its purpose. I want you to give it to Edward Valenti. It may take him a few minutes to grasp its import, but eventually he will understand and the fury will consume him." He saw Jeff's bewilderment and shook his head. "No. It isn't a map. There are no quick and easy instructions for the locating of buried treasure. It is, now, a fantastic, incredible and unintentional joke. I would like to see Edward's expression when he realizes what he holds in his hand." He paused.

"I am a very tired and very old man with the maggots of an unslaked longing for just one more drink of good bourbon gnawing at my vitals. Good night, Mr. Martin." The eyes closed.

Jeff went to the door and then turned. "Judge." He called softly. "I don't know how, but maybe you can let Judy know that I had to write this story because it couldn't be trusted to someone else, someone who wouldn't give a damn about her. I'd like her to know that it wasn't for a few bucks or for my job. She won't believe me if I tell her it would have been worse if I hadn't written it."

"Just the way I told it to you?"

"Just the way you told it to me."

"All right, Mr. Martin. I'll tell her. In return, should you come again while I am in this anteroom to the charnel house put a small flask in your hip pocket."

"I'll put two, Judge; one in each side. Good night."

Downstairs again he went to the head nurse's office and asked if she knew where Judy was staying. It was the Oleander Motel only a few blocks away.

Judy had stepped over the doorsill, out of the light behind her, in order to get a better look at the man who had knocked and now stood smiling pleasantly.

"Yes?" She had no explanation for the curious feeling of apprehension.

"I'm Doctor Fowler." The voice was quiet, soft and reassuring. "Resident at the County Hospital. I rang in a few minutes ago and, among other things, they told me your father has been asking for you. Since I had to pass here on my way to the hospital I thought I might give you a lift."

"Is he worse? Has something happened?"

"On the contrary." He was quietly reassuring. "That is why we indulge him. After all, it is late for visitors."

"Just a minute." She glanced behind her at the small room and then laughed self-consciously. "I don't know why I always have to look around before I leave."

"A feminine instinct for order." He was tolerantly amused.

Together they walked down a palm-shrouded path to where a car waited. As the doctor opened the rear door, holding it for her, she saw there was another passenger. He was a big man who leaned intently forward, as though searching for something up the street ahead. His heavy hands moved over each other with a massaging motion. He didn't turn or appear to be aware of her presence as she started to enter and something made her hesitate; an inexplicable, instinctive caution. She looked inquiringly at Dr. Fowler.

"An associate of mine." He took her arm and she had the odd impression that he was actually impelling her forward.

He closed the door and she sat stiffly and in wondering silence as the doctor moved behind the wheel. The big man still hadn't glanced at her. As the car rolled and gathered speed she again experienced a small, unaccountable prickle of something close to fear. She was worried without knowing why.

"Doctor."

"Yes?"

She attempted to make her words casual. "If you don't mind, I think I'd like to walk. It isn't far and I—I—well, I just like walking and it's such a nice night." She felt the first, small touch of panic. The car careened abruptly around a corner and leaped forward. "This is not the way to the hospital. You're no doctor." She attempted to beat at his shoulder.

"Hallie!" The driver spoke without turning.

"Yeah, Michael. Sure."

She was jerked back by a heavy hand and into a confining arm. The man's other hand clapped itself over her mouth, choking off her outcry. She struggled now with an intensity that had in it neither hysteria nor misdirection. It was a writhing, twisting fury. Her fingers raked the big man's face and she lashed out with her feet trying to reach him. Jerking her head to one side she managed to drive her teeth into a finger and she bit with the ferocity of a wounded animal until she felt her teeth gouge deep into the yielding flesh and the warm, sickeningly sweet taste of blood as it welled into her mouth. Still the man did not pull away his hand. She released her jaws, retching at the warm flood upon her tongue.

"She bit clear through my finger. How do you like that? Right clear through." Booker made the statement with something close to pride, as though an exceptionally accomplished child had performed for him.

For a second he released the pressure of his hand and she snapped her head back, freeing her mouth. She managed to scream once.

"Keep her quiet, Hallie."

"Yeah! Sure, Michael. Like you said. Keep her quiet." The heavy circle of his arm tightened until she thought her chest would cave in and the palm forced itself against her teeth until it seemed they would be pushed from their sockets. Still she tried to struggle. She butted his chin with her head and her foot caught him once in the shin.

"I sure don't like to hit no girl." Booker sighed. He tried to pin her down. "An' you ought to be more careful where you're goin', Michael. You can't steal a car in a small place like this without someone noticin'. If you want to steal a car then you gotta go some big place like New York, Kansas City, Des Moines. I fought in all them places."

To Judy as she continued to fight against him the words had the nightmarish quality of a drooling idiot chattering aimlessly. The effect was terrifying and she battled hysterically. Booker sighed again and then he turned her with surprising swiftness. The hard, bony edge of his hand clipped her viciously on the point of the jaw. It was a blow that carried with it no pain, only oblivion.

"I sure never liked to hit no girl," Booker said, as he allowed her to slide to the floor in a crumpled heap.

Jeff swung the car into the graveled driveway of the motel and drew to a halt where a sign spelled out the word office.

Inside, an elderly woman in a flowing dress of flowered crepe that looked as though it once might have served for a garden party turned from pouring coffee from a pot on a hot plate.

"Single or double?" She carried the cup over to the counter of varnished pine, pushed a registery card toward him and took a swallow of coffee. "I guess I make about the worst coffee on the whole East Coast." She added this cheerfully. "Never could figure out why." She regarded him brightly.

"Do you have a Miss Carter registered here?"

She put the cup down. "Who? Little Judy? Known her since she was a baby."

"Is she here?" His fingers drummed on the counter.

"You might say yes an', then again, you might say no. Usually I don't take in single girls. The goin's on an' all the extra towels they want. You know what I mean." She pursed her lips. "Men slippin' in an' out all the time. Think I don't see 'em but there's mighty little I don't know about. Got so now I can usually tell whether a couple's really married no matter how much luggage they got. My husband says it don't make no difference but I say if you're goin' to run a respectable place you got to keep an eye on things."

"Is Judy here?" he shouted, in an attempt to halt the flow of words.

"Don't you speak to me like that, young man." She was sharply reproving with a spinsterish quality. "I just got through tellin' you. I put little Judy, because I've known her since she was a baby, in Number Seven. New chintz curtains on the windows. I always say some bright chintz does wonders for a place."

He was at the door before her voice halted him.

"If you're goin' to Number Seven it won't do you no good. She ain't home. That's why I said you might say yes an' you might say no. She is here an' she ain't. A man come for her an' they went away together."

He wheeled in sudden alarm. "What man? Who was he?"

"You better learn some manners if you expect to get any place in this world. I was just watchin' from the window. I didn't go out an' ask his name. That there is Judy's business."

He strode to the counter and banged his fist on it. "Have you ever seen him before? What did he look like?"

"Young man, I just don't think I'll talk to you any more. Poundin' on the desk that way."

"Look." He kept his voice controlled. "This is important. What did the man look like?"

"Now! That's better. Ask a polite question an' you get a polite answer. Give an' take."

"For God's sake," he implored. "Will you please tell me what the man looked like?"

"Tch! Tch! The good Lord's name in vain."

"Please, Judy may be in trouble."

"Nobody gets into trouble here." She was superciliously amused. "But, I'll just humor you. This here was a tall, real thin man an' he wore horn-rimmed glasses. Looked real dignified, like a lawyer or maybe an undertaker. They talked for a minute an' then Judy an' him went to a car. There was another man in the car but I couldn't get a good look at him." Her mouth was open and remained that way as Jeff slammed the door behind him and disappeared. "Northerners! Always in a hurry." She picked up her cup. "This is sure bad coffee."

Bill Longworth, fully dressed but stretched out on the bed reading, answered the excited banging on his door and almost upon his invitation to enter it was flung open.

"Judy's gone. Spain and Booker picked her up at the motel. I don't know why she went with them. I told that damned old rumpot this would happen." Jeff's words came in a torrent of anger and concern.

The deputy swung his long legs over the side and stood up. "Good thing I decided to read instead of going to sleep as I intended."

"You're being pretty damned nonchalant about it, aren't you?"

"What do you want me to do, scream?"

Frustrated, Jeff watched as Longworth ran a comb through his hair, took a short jacket from the back of a chair and settled the light Stetson on his head. On his way to the door he carefully inserted a match tab at the place where he had finished reading and closed the book.

"Detective story." The admission was made with a small, embarrassed grin. "Pretty exciting stuff."

Neither spoke again until they were in the County car and racing down Main Street.

"At least we know where she is." Longworth whistled reflectively.

The words were so calmly reassuring, so confident and unworried that Jeff relaxed. "You're a good man to know." He made the statement with something close to admiration and affection. "A real, good man to know." He lit a cigarette.

"We'll pick up a boat at Norn's and go after her. This is kind of a break, Martin. For me, I mean. This I can nail them on. All I had before was a motive for the Hathaway killing." As though he sensed Jeff's protest he continued unhurriedly. "They won't hurt her. They're after the judge. She's just bait—live bait."

"I guess you're right." Jeff was beginning to feel a little foolish over his display of panic.

Longworth skidded to a stop before Norn's dock. The rooms above the tackle shop were dark. As they started to leave the car the deputy unlocked the glove compartment and took from it a stubby 38-caliber revolver. He checked the cylinder and filled chambers and handed it to Jeff.

"Know how to use it?"

"Sure. You just hold it out in front of you. Shut your eyes. Pull this little thing and it goes boom! boom! boom!"

"That's the general idea." Longworth was already on his way to Norn's. "Don't use it unless you have to. The bad one is Spain. Booker is a trained gorilla."

They awoke Norn, who was sleepy and querulously angry until he recognized Longworth. He pulled a pair of dungarees on over the long underwear in which he had been sleeping. Padding in his bare feet and holding a flashlight to guide them, he led the way to the small mooring basin.

"What do you want, Sheriff, an outboard?"

"No-o-o. Give me something a little bigger. Maybe that over there. I figure we'll, maybe, have some passengers on the way back."

CHAPTER THIRTEEN

*J*udy stood in the center of the room, straight and proudly defiant. Her jaw ached intolerably but she refused to betray the hurt by so much as touching her hand to the sore spot.

It was a curious tableau. Michael Spain, in a wicker rocker beneath a white china shaded oil lamp, reading with scholarly detachment, turning the pages of his book with a meditative air. Doris, in electric-blue lounging pyjamas, the blouse deliberately unbuttoned to the deep cleft of her breasts, lay upon her back on a couch blowing smoke rings at the ceiling. Booker, with the hungry appearance of a devoted mastiff, stared at her from a nearby chair. When she moved, throwing one long leg over another, he shifted uneasily. In a yellow robe of terry cloth Marcia stood by a front window, idly peeling an orange. Only Valenti was restless and this he betrayed by the constant thrusting of his hands into his pockets and withdrawing them.

"I don't know you." Judy's eyes were fired by anger. "I never saw any of you before. You have nothing to do with me so why have I been brought here? What do you want?"

Booker clasped and unclasped his hands and leaned forward.

"Gee! You do that swell, Dorrie. Makin' smoke rings." He devoured her with his eyes.

She rolled over sinuously to smile at him. "That isn't the only thing I do well, Buster."

"Isn't anyone going to answer me?" Judy had the feeling she was in a madhouse.

"Now why don't you be a good girl?" Valenti was patient. "No one is going to hurt you. Let's just say you are our guest."

"Ha!" Doris uttered the single exclamation heavily larded with sarcasm. She left the couch with a fluid grace and in passing Booker's chair allowed her fingers to trail across his cheek and ear. He shivered, his eyes never leaving her as she walked to a table on which were Scotch, a bottle of sherry, glasses and water. "Ha! Again." She poured herself a straight drink, downed it with a shudder then turned to Judy with bright interest. "If you're a guest, sister, you're in for some real fun. See? Not even ice."

"I never knew that a broad, even a dumb one, could get on my nerves so." A small muscle jumped near Valenti's eye. "I'm sick of the sound of your voice."

"Then let me out of this trap." She deliberately goaded him.

Marcia regarded the blonde speculatively. Doris was too smart not to know what she was doing. Marcia wondered why. There was the open display of her body which she had been flaunting in front of Booker all evening until the big hulk had been reduced to helpless longing. He was ready to get down on his knees and lick her feet. Now she was working Valenti into an uncontrollable rage. Again Marcia wondered why.

"I don't want to be your guest," Judy shouted.

"And I don't blame you, sister," Doris approved. "No ice."

Valenti's eyes were black agates of rage. His hands trembled as he thrust them again into his pockets. "When I get things off my mind I'm personally going to beat the hell out of you."

"And boy, do I ever love it." She rocked her pelvis with lewd insinuation. "It sends me Daddy-o!"

Booker licked his lips with a dry tongue and Doris stared at him with slumberously hot passion; her eyes half closed, her wet mouth partly open.

Valenti strode across the room and back and Michael Spain lowered his book for a moment to watch. At some time during those years in prison Valenti had lost his nerve. He cowered a little now behind a façade but the real Valenti was gone. The icy deadliness was melting, had melted. Now, when he should be cold, calculating every risk, weighing every chance, planning his moves, he was being reduced to insensate fury by this girl.

"You keep quiet. Do you hear?" Valenti's finger wavered visibly as he pointed it at Doris.

"I want to know why I am here? Why I was beaten and thrown into a boat?" Judy persisted.

"You keep quiet, too. I tell all of you. This is Valenti." The voice was guttural and almost accented. "Tomorrow we send a little note to the judge." He drew a deep breath and seemed to get himself under control. "We say you are visiting us and wouldn't he, maybe, like to join us. The judge and I used to be good friends. We got a lot of things to talk over."

"I don't believe you." She was scornful. "He wouldn't have anything to do with hoodlums like you."

A puzzled alertness crept into Valenti's expression as she spoke. His head cocked a little to one side like an inquisitive terrier.

"You look like someone I know." The words came slowly as he searched his memory, groping through the labyrinth of time. "Who does she look like, Michael?"

Spain regarded her across the top of his book. "Just a girl." He resumed his reading.

"See what I mean, sister?" Doris reached again for the Scotch. "They know what a girl looks like around this trap even if they don't know what one is for."

Valenti's hand swung out and sent her glass crashing against the wall. "You lay off that stuff, hear?" He glared at her. "A fresh quiff like you interrupting Valenti."

Doris's gaze went beyond him to Booker as he half rose from his chair, and there was the faintest of knowing smiles around her full mouth as she saw this first, tentative and uncertain indication of rebellion. Just a little more and he'd go, even though he sank back now in fumbling indecision.

Judy was puzzled by what she felt rather than saw. It was charged with tension. The air was as heavy as a storm cloud before lightning slashes through it. There was a strange, controlled but deadly menace in the room.

"Now look. We got to stay here together. I don't want any more foolishness." Valenti's words were an odd combination of command and plea. "Maybe we get on each others' nerves. So, we got to stand it. Now." He made an attempt to smile. "We all have a drink and Hal will fix a late snack. He's a good cook, aren't you, Hallie?"

Ordinarily Booker would have displayed a slavish gratitude for a word of commendation from the great man. Now, he sat and stared sullenly at the floor, his slow mind filled with a creeping resentment. Valenti was too preoccupied to notice or accept the big man's absence of a reply as a warning. Spain did. He lowered his book and studied Booker and then his glance shifted to Valenti. He watched the nervous tic and saw the man's hands clasp and unclasp and then lift to rub at a strained face. Michael carefully placed his book on the table. Marcia, also, was aware of what was happening. Her mouth pursed thoughtfully and she laid the peeled orange on the window sill and dropped her hands into the large pockets of the heavy robe. Doris turned on the radio and as the music issued from the speaker Valenti nodded his approval.

"That's a good girl, Dorrie. I forgive you for being so fresh. We'll have some music and a little drink."

She turned her back on him and, going to the table, poured herself another Scotch.

"Get me a little sherry, Dorrie."

Turning, glass in hand, she stared at him for a moment. There was an insolent curve to her mouth and then she deliberately took the straight drink and stood looking at him.

"Get it yourself!"

For one terrible moment there was no sound and then into the vacuum the hissing intake of breath as Valenti drew it between his teeth. It was as sinister as the warning rattle of a snake. There was a reptilian change in Valenti himself. His neck appeared to grow longer, his head smaller as it was thrust forward, weaving as though the bared teeth were fangs with which to strike. Doris stood waiting, actually inviting what she knew must happen. When his hand flew out, beating her across the face, she staggered and flinched but did not back away.

"You dirty little whore!" The words were strained and pitched in an insane key. "You cheap tramp. You speak to Valenti that way?"

"Don't hit Dorrie no more." Booker was on his feet. His body swayed, rocking with the motion of an uneasy elephant. The small eyes burned with a faintly reddish light and the mouth twitched and twisted as the lips formed soundless words. The long arms and heavy hands were loose and shaking and the fingers opened and closed as though they were things apart.

For a second Valenti seemed not to have heard and then he whirled to face Booker. "You dummy!" he screamed. "You cheap punk. I've hired your kind by the dozens just to wipe my shoes."

"Don't hit Dorrie no more. She's my girl." There was an idiotic intensity about the repetition and the dull voice was made more frightening by its monotone. His feet shuffled but they did not propel him forward.

"Don't hit Dorrie?" A bubble of froth appeared on Valenti's lips. "You punchy slob. I'll show you whether I'll hit Dorrie again." He spun and struck her full across the mouth with the back of his hand. "I'll kill you both for this." The hand lashed out again.

There was the power of ungoverned fury behind the last blow. It knocked Doris back. She stumbled and fell, crumpling into a corner. A crimson thread trailed from the corner of her mouth and she dazedly lifted her fingers and pulled at it while her terror-filled gaze never left Booker's face.

The big man was moving now. Slowly, with a flat-footed, relentless glide. "I told you not to hit Dorrie no more. Sure I told you. You know that. Nobody hits Dorrie no more." There was a stubborn absence of emphasis in the statement.

"Keep away from him, Booker." Marcia's command was a lash and it had the effect of a pony's whip on a rhinoceros.

For the first time Valenti appeared to realize what he had set in motion. His eyes darted from Booker to Spain and he wet his lips with quick nervousness, backing against the small table as the sliding gait continued. The distance that could have been covered in a few strides was made to seem interminable and unendurable by the big man's dragging progress. He was intent upon only one thing and it seemed to make no difference to him how long it took. He was something out of primordial slime, half-beast, half-man, who had as yet learned only to kill.

Valenti screamed. It was a shrill, quavering note of terror. His eyes sought an avenue of escape and found none. He screamed again, compressing himself against the table's edge.

"Michael! Michael!"

Spain did not move from his chair.

"Booker! Keep away from him." Again it was Marcia's voice but the man only shook his head as though he had been struck and would clear it. She was cold, watching him almost dispassionately and then her hand came out of the robe's pocket and with it Hathaway's revolver. "Booker!"

The first slug tore into his guts but it did not halt him. He only turned, a puzzled question in his eyes as they fastened upon her. Then, as if he were some great beast set upon by pygmy tormenters, he lumberingly changed direction, moving upon her.

The second slug hit him in the chest and for a second there was pain and surprise on his face but he did not halt, continuing with the relentless progress of a prehistoric monster.

The third bullet hit him in the throat and for one horrible moment he stood, nailed, as the blood spurted, the great vein pumping a crimson froth that sprayed itself upon him and the floor. Then, as a stricken thing, he pitched forward, his length and momentum carrying his head close to her feet and what was left of Hal Booker ran out, painting the hem of her yellow robe with a scarlet dye.

Longworth and Jeff were just beyond the pierhead when the night was cracked open by the sound of revolver shots. The deputy threw the throttle full up, cutting it only at the last moment and the prow of the craft lifted and slid up on the soft bank. Almost before it touched he was out and running with Jeff pounding behind him.

In the corner, her head lolling, hair trailing over her face, Doris vomited uncontrollably. Judy, incredulous horror in her eyes, had pressed her back to the far wall and stood there transfixed, unable to believe what she had seen; unable to run or cry out.

Valenti chattered insanely. "You were goin' to let him do it, Michael. You just sat there. You didn't try to stop him. You wanted him to get me, didn't you? With me out of the way you have it all to yourself. Only this one, a dame I hardly know, stopped him."

"Oh, shut up." Marcia spat the words contemptuously. "You're no good to me dead. He could have pulled your arms and legs off for all I care." With one foot she carelessly pushed the bloody head away from her robe.

Longworth and Jeff, guns in hand, burst through the back door and at the living room's entrance halted at the spectacle. Then, as the deputy stood, the grey of his eyes flinty with a hard anger, Valenti began to shake with an uncontrollable chill.

"She did it." He pointed an accusing finger. "I liked the boy. I wouldn't harm him."

Jeff went to Judy. "Are you all right?" She nodded dumbly but there was gratitude in her eyes and when he put his arm around her shoulders she sagged a little and he could feel her tremble with a sudden spasm. "Take it easy." He continued soothingly. "You'll be all right now."

"I'll take the gun." Longworth's voice was as level as his eyes as he spoke to Marcia.

"That's the only way you'll get it." She was rebellious for a second and then shrugged. "No. I guess you're right. Here." She tossed him the revolver.

He caught it in the left hand, holding his own gun in the other. Then, still watching Spain he pushed Valenti hard against the table, searching him quickly.

"I don't carry a gun. You ought to know that." Some of Valenti's courage and arrogance returned. "I got punks for that."

"You." Longworth motioned to Spain. "Up against the wall."

Michael turned slowly, reluctantly. His hands were high, palms pressed against the boards. Longworth went over him and took away a .32 automatic.

"All right." He stepped back and surveyed them with bitter satisfaction. "It's just too damn bad I can't let you alone to kill each other off and save the state a lot of money." Out of the corner of his eye he caught a movement by Doris as she straightened and stood up shakily. "Go wash your face. You look like hell."

"Yes, sir." She was meek and grateful.

"Now." The deputy continued. "While we're all together I want to know who killed Hathaway?"

"Michael!" Valenti loosed the word and there was the venom of satisfaction on his tongue. "Michael and Booker." He smiled wolfishly at Spain. "I told them not to lean on him hard."

Longworth shook his head wearily. "You're a real boy for the choir, aren't you? I don't know." His glance traveled over them. "None of you ever learn. Half your lives are spent in prisons and the other half dodging and hiding from the law and decent people and you still think you're the smart ones. Even when you make a big take you never get a chance to spend it. Maybe I'm dumb but I can't figure the percentage."

"We'll get you a platform and a revival tent, Sheriff." Marcia was scornful.

Longworth took one of the straw rugs and tossed it over Booker. As he turned away Doris came back and he nodded as though he were pleased by the change in her appearance.

"All right. Let's go." Then, recalling something, he turned to Jeff. "You told me that Cartright gave you something for Valenti?"

"Yeah! I almost forgot. Here." He crossed the room and handed Valenti the square of oiled silk.

Valenti took it suspiciously. "What the hell is this, some sort of a joke?"

"I don't know," Jeff was cheerfully alert. "Judge Cartright said you would. He said he'd like to see your face when you opened it. So open it and let's take a look at your face. Then I'll tell him about it."

Slowly, Valenti's fingers worked at the fabric but his eyes darted from Longworth to Jeff. He bit on his lip and then, as though hypnotized, he folded back the final silken tab. Creased there was a hundred-dollar bill. Valenti took it by both ends, opening it out. It made no sense to Jeff and he glanced inquiringly at the deputy and was surprised to see the beginning of a grin crinkle around his eyes. Valenti stared at the bill and then he began to laugh, only it wasn't a laugh. It was an insane gurgling, a scream and a whimper in which there was agony and frustration.

"See what we got, Michael?" The bill dangled limply as he thrust it with a quivering hand for Spain's inspection. "A million an' a quarter dollars in this. These old, big bills, the ones they took out of circulation when they issued the small ones. You couldn't spend it, Michael, not a dollar. With these you walk into a bank and you might as well have a sign around your neck. Stolen. A hell of a big joke, huh, Michael." The laughter grew hysterical. "Over a million dollars and they might as well be in Confederate money. All the time the judge knew this." Tears began to spill down his cheeks. He screamed at Spain. "It's all your damned fault. Years ago when we could have cashed them I told you from prison. Find Cartright, he has the money. Only, you're too Goddamned dumb. You have to wait until Valenti gets out to find him for you. Now it's no good. I spit on you and your mother. I wish you to burn in hell." He wiped at the tears with the back of one hand and then began to laugh again, an idiotic cackling that filled the room with madness.

Longworth stepped forward and slapped him across the face, hard. The blow shocked him to a return of sanity but his body continued to shake.

"We'll go now." The deputy glanced at Doris and Marcia. "You'd better get some clothes on."

"This will do." Marcia dug out a cigarette, lit it and inhaled deeply. Then she almost smiled. "I figure I'll get a new wardrobe from the state anyhow."

"Jesus! My trousseau!" Doris wailed. "I got a lot of clothes, new ones, stuff I never got to wear."

"Take what you can carry." He turned away indifferently. "But let's get the show on the road."

CHAPTER FOURTEEN

*J*eff **leaned back** from the typewriter they had loaned him in the Western Union office at West Palm Beach, pulled the final sheet from the machine and handed it to the attendant with a sigh of relief.

He had been writing steadily, giving the story in short takes to the operator for transmission. Now, his mouth was dry from too many cigarettes, his eyes red from the strain and lack of sleep but within him there was the warm glow of satisfaction. It was a hell of a story, a clean beat and he had nursed it along from the beginning to its bloody end.

He stood up, stretched, yawned and halted for a moment behind the operator as the final paragraph was being sent. The man looked over his shoulder with a grin.

"Real mystery story, huh?"

"You said it. A real mystery story. Dames, dough, shooting, the works. Thanks a lot for your help."

He went outside, standing in the cool, fresh hour before dawn. In the quiet he could hear the soft, rolling murmur of the ocean on the other side of Lake Worth. It was going to be a fine day and he was sitting right on top of it. He rested his arms on the convertible's top, bowing his head between them. Shutting his eyes he could see the *Globe*'s city room at this hour. The lobster trick in and the spasmodic clatter of a typewriter now and then. The thump of the leather cylinders as they came through the pneumatic tube with proofs from the composing room. Old man Wentworth, with his clips from the morning papers, passing them out to rewrite for the paper's early Home Edition. Ford, in the slot of the copy desk and the green-shaded men along the rim, writing heads and making corrections in copy. Ford had probably called Grant as the first of the Cartright story began to come in and Burrows would have telephoned the Old Man. Between them they had decided on the front page make-up and by now it was all geared to go. They'd hit the street early and in a few hours every city desk in New York would be in an uproar.

"You Pulitzer Prize bastard, you." He grinned to himself and straightened up. He'd find a lunchroom, get some breakfast and go back to the Cay.

After Longworth had called the hospital and made arrangements for Judy to have a room next to the judge he had driven her there. It had been a different Judy, quiet, subdued and inclined to press close to him on the front seat. He had kissed her good night and she had clung, whispering meaningless, tender words.

"I'll come and get you in the morning, after I get back from Palm Beach."

"You're going to write it?" Her face clouded momentarily.

"Of course I'm going to write it. Do you think it can be kept a secret? The judge understands. He'll tell you."

"All right, Jeff." Her eyes softened. "Come for me soon. I'm lonely without you."

He had gone back to Norn's Dock where Longworth and his prisoners waited for additional cars and deputies. Someone would have to go back to the house and stay with Booker until the medical examiner arrived. Valenti and Spain, silent, bitter and filled with hatred for each other, were handcuffed together in the back seat of Longworth's car. Marcia, still in the blood-stained robe, stood near it, scornfully aloof and silent. Doris, shivering a little in the lounging pyjamas, stared hopefully up at the deputy.

"What about me, Sheriff?" She was plaintive.

"Well, what about you?" Longworth blew upon the coal of his cigarette.

"What I mean is—well I'm just a kid who came along for the ride. You know I didn't have anything to do with the shooting of Booker and the Hathaway business."

"You'll probably get fifteen or twenty years as an accessory."

"You're kidding." Her eyes were wide. "Tell me you're kidding."

As he looked at her the tiny lines around his eyes that were always the beginning of that quiet, shy smile, appeared. "I'm kidding." He acknowledged. "They'll hold you as a material witness."

"You mean I have to go to the pokey?"

"Uh-huh."

"For how long?"

"That depends." His gaze traveled over her appreciatively. "You're quite a dish. I said it the first time I saw you. A real dish."

"Well!" Her confidence returned. This she could understand. "That's better. It's been a hell of a long time since anyone seemed to notice it. I didn't figure you were human."

"I'm human enough." He arched the cigarette away.

"Do I really have to go to the pokey?" Without seeming to move she was, somehow, closer to him and he could feel the fragrant warmth of her body through the sheer fabric. "I didn't do anything."

"Well. I just might get you released into my custody until the trial."

"How long would that be?"

He shrugged. "I don't know. Months, maybe."

"What will I do? Where would I stay?" There was small laughter in her eyes now.

"I guess you'd have to stay with me. That is, if we're going to have real protective custody."

"I like the sound of that." She lifted her face and her eyes were luminous.

The other cars arrived then and Jeff had followed them into West Palm Beach.

Now, on the sidewalk with daybreak fanning out in great golden fingers on the horizon, he decided he didn't want any breakfast. He only wanted to get back to the Cay and Judy.

She was sitting alone in the hospital room, seeming small and abjectly pitiful. He could see that she had been crying but the tears were gone now and only her eyes betrayed a deep and brooding sadness. He lifted her from the chair and she pressed against him.

"He's dead, Jeff. He died about half an hour after I got here. The doctors couldn't do anything. He just didn't want to live. He told me that." She lifted her face from his chest and stared at him. "He told me to trust you." She tried to smile. "He said you were a good man. He told me a lot of things, but he didn't tell me who I am. Who am I, Jeff?"

His arms tightened, drawing her close again. "You're my girl."

After a moment he could feel her head move against him with a gesture of assent. "That's good enough for me."

They drove from the hospital to the waterfront and out along the marsh to the creek where the houseboat was moored.

"I don't think I want to go aboard just now, Jeff. It hurts too much."

"It's pretty well torn up, but I guess it can be fixed. I don't know much about those things but a good carpenter ought to be able to do it."

"What does that mean?" She turned within the circle of his arm, her eyes shining.

"You didn't think I was going back to New York without you?"

"I hoped not." Her voice was small.

"I don't think you'd be happy there. I don't think I'd like it much myself after this. I'll go down to Miami in a couple of days and see about a job."

"I'm pretty inexpensive, Jeff. Besides, we have my boat. Fish and grits aren't so bad if you throw in a little side meat and turnip greens now and then."

"I'll do better than that for you. I'm a real red-hot newspaperman today."

"Oh!" She covered her mouth to shut off the exclamation. "I almost forgot." She dug into a pocket of her skirt. "Pop gave me this for you."

It was a short note, scrawled in a shaky and uneven hand but it told him where the money could be found, in a couple of trunks in the attic of a house in a small, remote village in the Catskills.

He stepped on the starter and swung the car about.

"Is it important?"

"Yes, I suppose it is. I'll give it to Burrows over the phone. It will make a hell of a follow-up for tomorrow."

She studied his face gravely. "I don't know whether I'll like being a reporter's wife. You go away from me when something happens."

"What makes you think I'm going to marry you?"

"Well, aren't you?" She leaned forward to study him.

"I don't know." He was casually indifferent. "When I came down here Burrows said the place was filled with native girls wearing lotus blossoms in their hair."

"How are the natives, Mr. Christian, asked Captain Bligh?"

He put his arm about her shoulders, drawing her close. "Friendly, sir. Very friendly indeed."